Longarm wanted to know who was following him, and how come.

He strode towards the hotel, trying to act neither hurried nor suspicious until he got to the next corner, ducked around it, and backed into the shade of some side stairs as he clunked in place to sound as if he was still going.

It worked. Those high-heeled boots came around the corner on the double as Longarm tried to duplicate the sound of bootheels fading away in the distance. So then it was a simple matter of reaching out to grab a fistful of shirt, swing the cuss around to slam into the painted pine siding, and shove a gun muzzle in his face for him to smell.

"You've caught up with me at last, you sly son of a bitch," growled Longarm. "And now you're fixing to tell me what you had in mind if you'd like your brains to remain in your skull this evening."

TABOR EVANS

LONGARM

AND THE
JOHN BULL FEUD

JOVE BOOKS, NEW YORK

LONGARM AND THE JOHN BULL FEUD

A Jove Book/published by arrangement with
the author

PRINTING HISTORY
Jove edition/July 1995

ISBN: 0-515-11655-6

A JOVE BOOK®
Jove Books are published by The Berkley Publishing Group,
200 Madison Avenue, New York, New York 10016.
JOVE and the "J" design are trademarks
belonging to Jove Publications, Inc.

PRINTED IN THE UNITED STATES OF AMERICA

10 9 8 7 6 5 4 3 2 1

Chapter 1

That gent who described the road to hell as paved with good intentions knew his onions. Deputy U.S. Marshal Custis Long intended a good turn for a fellow lawman as he made his way along a marble corridor of the Denver Federal Building with his tobacco-brown frock coat neatly buttoned over the grips of the .44-40 he was packing, cross-draw, on his left hip.

The tall dark deputy paused outside an oak-paneled door and got out a three-for-a-nickel cheroot, knowing how offensive some found that brand. He lit it with a wax-stemmed Mexican match and strode into his own home office with the long skinny smoke gripped at a jaunty angle by his innocent grin.

Young Henry, the pallid clerk they had playing that typewriter out front, shot a thoughtful glance at the wall clock as he tried not to retch like a schoolmarm. He swallowed hard and said primly, "You're supposed to be pulling courtroom duty down at the far end of the premises. If you've come to argue the point with our Marshal Vail, you just missed him. Didn't he tell you he had to attend that out-of-town political powwow for the rest of this week?"

Their mutual boss sure had. Longarm, as he was better known to many a friend or foe, had been watching from behind a handy pillar out front as the fair but firm Billy Vail had driven off for Union Station in a hired hack. Longarm hated to get cussed out by such a skilled grump when his heart was pure.

He blew some more smoke Henry's way and grabbed a handy bentwood chair to swing it around and settle astraddle across the desk from the green-faced clerk. "Smiley and Dutch are riding herd on that miscreant Judge Dickerson's fixing to hang for getting so forward with an Indian agent's wife," Longarm said.

Henry shot another confused glance at that wall clock and asked in an injured tone, "Can't anybody read the plain English I'm sure I typed out on this very machine? Smiley and Dutch are supposed to be at least as far west as Lookout Mountain even as we speak. The town law at a mining camp called John Bull is holding a federal want for us. Marshal Vail told me to send Smiley and Dutch to fetch him."

Longarm nodded, exhaled more pungent tobacco smoke, and replied, "That's what I wanted to talk to the boss about. But you'll do just as fine, seeing you get to type up all them swell field orders."

Henry just looked bewildered. So Longarm continued. "You must've heard about old Smiley busting up with that hot-tempered breed gal a spell back. His disposition's improved a heap since he's found his true love waiting on tables at Pfeiffer's Beer Garden."

Henry waved some papers between them as if to get a clearer view of Longarm as he grimaced and said, "I've seen her. Every man to his own taste, and Smiley was in here before you, trying to talk Marshal Vail into sending someone else so he could squire his new sweetie to that cake sale and dance at the Grange Hall this evening. The stenographer ladies down the way sent us a formal complaint about what Smiley said, with the words they found most shocking typed out in dashes."

Longarm nodded soberly and replied, "Smiley don't know how you reason with such a strict public servant as Billy Vail. *I told* him how you can't change orders typed in triplicate just to squire a pretty gal to a shindig. You have to sweeten the pot with a change of value to the government, as I was hoping to had I caught up with the boss before he lit out on us."

Henry frowned thoughtfully and said, "Picking up and transporting a petty crook and possible informant sounded simple enough as I was taking down Marshal Vail's instructions. You get off the broad-gauge at Golden, transfer to the narrow-gauge running beyond Lookout Mountain, and ride, say, thirty miles by crow. I'd say it had to be a tad farther by hairpin turns through the Front Range, but we're not talking about bringing back Doctor Livingston from darkest Africa."

Longarm said, "That's doubtless why Billy Vail assigned the two of 'em. I reckon you know why the boss likes to team Smiley and Dutch?"

Henry nodded. "That's no mystery. Smiley could track a swan across a lake if said swan had a federal warrant out on it. But Smiley can't draw half as fast as the deadly but sort of dumb Dutch. So either one can get in trouble working alone. But with both of them working together, they add up to smarter and faster than anyone they're likely to run up against."

Henry waved more smoke out of his face as he added, "What are you smoking, a buzzard quill? The two of them were assigned to go fetch that half-baked young train robber because Marshal Vail and Judge Dickerson want to talk to him about the whereabouts of his older and meaner pals and that's *that,* you smoldering dung heap!"

Longarm said, "A deputy in the field draws six cents a

mile. His prisoner draws the same. That means Smiley and Dutch will be allowed twelve cents a mile going and eighteen cents a mile all the way back from John Bull.''

Henry snorted. ''Gee, thanks. I never would have been able to work out by payday.''

Longarm pushed on. ''I wasn't planning on going to that Grange Hall this evening. It's sort of tedious when a man bids on one gal's cake and another one cries. So if I was to swap details with Smiley and Dutch, it would cost the taxpayers only six cents a mile one way and twelve the other. I ain't talking crow miles neither. Them hairpin miles add up in the Front Range. So how's about it, old son?''

Henry shook his head and said, ''I follow your drift, and we both know Vail's a Scotch name. But do I have the authority to change a superior's orders without asking?''

Longarm tried, ''We can say you asked *me*. I'm the superior lawman within earshot now that the cat's away. If old Billy ain't pleased as punch by the way you figured out how to save all that money for the government, you can blame it all on me, see?''

Henry could. As he put fresh onionskins and carbon paper in his machine he observed, ''I heard about that friendly little game over at the House of Detention during the death watch of the late Roger Palechester. How much did Smiley get into you for, seeing you're so anxious to change places with him on a dancing night in June?''

To which Longarm could only reply, ''Enough,'' with as sheepish a smile as he could muster. For he figured it might sound mushy if a grown man allowed he felt he owed another just for saving his life one time. And what the hell, whipping over to pick up one dumb kid and getting him back to Denver in one piece didn't sound like such a hard row to hoe. Longarm intended to have Smiley's chore finished by the time their boss got back from his own train ride.

4

Chapter 2

Golden, Colorado, had been the territorial capital until 1867, when they've moved the seat of government to handier and flatter ground a few miles east and called it Denver. What was left sort of lazed in a hammock formed by the aprons of the fair-sized Lookout Mountain and the way smaller but more dramatic red sandstone butte called Castle Rock. The mines that had brought the foothill town into being were about played out, but Golden hung on as a satellite town of its big fat daughter, Denver, thanks to its spring water and the ever-growing local market for beer.

The well water of Denver was too hard to brew good beer, and nobody with a lick of sense drank from the polluted South Platte or Cherry Creek as they joined near the Denver Stockyards. But ideal beer water sprang abundantly from the quartz roots of the Front Range, and barley just right for malting seemed to thrive where little else would, in the thin dry air where the High Plains swept up as grassy hogbacks to form the doorsteps of the Rocky Mountains. So there was still enough work to feed around four thousand souls, and a spur of the C&SRR ran over from Denver to fetch and carry for them.

Longarm got off the broad-gauge combination with no baggage, even though he was nowhere near his final destination. He liked to travel light, and he knew they had at least one hotel where he could stay the night in the even smaller mining town he was aiming for. It was only transfer layovers and turnaround time that old Smiley had been worried about to begin with. The round trip alone wouldn't have added up to a full work day away from the office and Grange dances, if you didn't have to spend more than half your travel time waiting for some other damned train to carry you another few damned miles. It made Longarm wish they'd get cracking with that horseless carriage they promised he'd see someday if only he'd keep reading the *Scientific American.*

It was now just after noon, without a cloud in the sky or a hint of moisture in the thin dry air. So Longarm consulted his watch and crunched off across the traprock ballast of the Golden rail yards as he idly wondered why it always smelled like a cobwebbed hayloft over in these foothills, indoors or out. The big dust-colored and butterfly-winged grasshoppers he seemed to be chasing across the bare stone, sun-silvered cross ties, and warm steel rails were another mystery. He always flushed the big bugs in warm weather as he cut across bone-dry yards or vacant lots. He'd yet to figure out what giant grasshoppers were *doing* where there wasn't a blade of grass in sight.

He didn't know such wondering habits made him as dangerous to the riders of the owlhoot trail as his fast draw and steady aim. He knew he'd solved more than one crime by recalling some hitherto useless bit of information he'd picked up and filed away as he wandered a world filled with wonders. But he was sure he'd never need any help from those rail yard grasshoppers, even as he filed away yet another dumb bug springing up from a switch point with a flash of its black and yellow wings. He was crossing the narrow-gauge rails of these modest yards now. He knew how they shoved or shoveled loads from broad- or narrow-gauge cars parked side by side. He knew the one-yard-wide narrow-gauge track could carry a dinkier train over giddy trestles and around mountain hairpins no man-sized train would dare on wheels set almost five feet apart. But he couldn't figure out why the smaller tracks of this particular narrow-gauge were fastened to their cross ties in such a complicated way.

Like most self-educated men, Longarm tended to be a jack of all such interesting detail and a master of none. But he felt sure most of the narrow-gauge mountain track he'd noticed in his time had only been a smaller and if anything simpler version of plain old railroad track, with the broader bottom flange of the Stevens or All American rail either floating on flat steel cushions or spiked directly to the ties. This line that meant to carry him on up to John Bull one of these days seemed to be set as expensively as all get-out, with a sort of small steel vice gripping the bottom flange of lighter rail from each and every cross tie.

Longarm was on the far side of the yard and pushing through some trackside bugleweed toward the Mexican *cafetín* he'd re-called in these parts when he suddenly nodded to himself and, without bothering to look back, said aloud, "Well, sure, they *told* you the place was named John Bull to begin with!"

He'd read somewhere how some Englishmen had in-vented the steam locomotive just before the Prophet Joseph invented the Mormons in York State, back around '27. See-ing they hadn't had to run railroads in England for long distances, the whole country fitting into Colorado with room to spare, they'd had no call to keep up with refine-ments such as the far less expensive Stevens rail, air brakes, Janney coupler, and such. The little he knew about the sil-ver camp at the far end of those narrow-gauged but fancy tracks said the original strike had been developed by a syndicate of British investors. It stood to reason a bunch of mining engineers from England would lay tracks the way they'd been taught in their old country. He figured it had cost them three or for times as much for every twisty mile. But fair was fair, and it did seem less likely they'd derail on some lonesome hairpin with the tracks gripped so securely by all those bitty steel bulldog jaws.

As he entered the sudden shade of the trackside *cafetín*, he could only guess at what the lady seated at the counter with a couple of kids might really look like. Her voice seemed nice enough, considering, as she tried in vain to order broth and soda crackers from the willing but sincerely puzzled Mexican lady on the other side of the counter.

Ticking the brim of his Stetson as he deliberately took a seat a couple of stools down, Longarm declared, "I'd be of honest intent and some knowledge of the Spanish lingo if you all could use a hand, ma'am. After that, I ain't sure they serve either broth or soda crackers here. You and your young'ns have strayed into what we call a *cafetín* because it ain't half fancy enough to be called a cafe. If none of you are familiar with Mex cooking, I suggest you let me order you some *arroz con pollo*, which tastes like plain American grub, only more so, with some *tortillas*, which are sort of a cross betwixt pancakes and soda crackers, in taste at least."

The gal hesitated, then said she'd just had the boy's tonsils out in Denver and wasn't sure he was up to anything spicy yet.

Longarm was too polite to ask her why in thunder she'd hauled the kid into a Mexican restaurant before his throat had taken the time to heal. He said, "I'm fixing to order for the three of you then. It's on me. So just don't eat it if you can't stand it."

She started to protest, but Longarm was already explaining it all to the fatter Mexican gal, and she agreed in a motherly way that a kid with a raw throat would do better on a double helping of *cascos de guayaba con queso,* while the two ladies might fancy more modest servings of *arroz con pollo,* seeing they were new at the game. When he ordered *huevos rancheros* for himself, the Mexican lady chuckled fondly and said she saw he wasn't.

Then she said, *"Se necesita un cuarto de hora,"* and waddled off to fill their orders as Longarm noticed for the first time that the Anglo gal he'd orderd for wasn't half bad-looking.

Her auburn hair was swept up under a straw spring boater, and her summer-weight blue calico dress went swell with her wide-set eyes. The half-grown boy and girl she had in tow favored her cameo features, but they seemed a mite old to be her own. Instead of saying so, Longarm told her, "They need a quarter hour here to whip up anything but regular hot chili, ma'am. I hope the three of you have that time to spare."

She dimpled at him, and replied she and her two young charges had to catch the same afternoon train up to John Bull. Going to the big town to have your tonsils out or going to the small town to pick up a federal want involved the same tedious layover in the middle-sized town they were stuck in.

The young boy wanted to know what they'd be asked to eat within a quarter hour. Longarm explained, "The two ladies with you will have a chicken and rice dish that ain't as unusual to their tastes as, say, chicken baked in bitter chocolate, or hot tamales. In view of your own delicate state, I ordered you a sort of hearty dessert made out of fruit preserves and cottage cheese."

Longarm could see he hadn't hurt the ten-or eleven-year-old gal's feelings by describing her as a lady. So he asked her directly what she'd like to wash her grub down with.

The young gal blushed and allowed she'd like some coffee with her grub. The older gal, to her credit, just smiled knowingly and allowed they'd all have the same, with extra cream. Longarm didn't want to discuss goat's milk or worse. So he only warned them they'd likely get the condensed kind as he made a mental note to ask the old Mexican gal to bust open a can no matter what it might cost.

By the time the fat lady got back with their platters so he could tell her that, and so he could order *café negro* for his own fried eggs with pepper sauce, raw onion, grated cheese, and Lord only knows what else, he'd learned the pretty young gal was the older sister of the two kids. She'd allowed her name was Flora Munro, but that she had no idea why one needed pot holders served with otherwise sensible-looking grub.

Longarm chuckled and explained, "They ain't pot holders, ma'am. I told you they'd serve you tortillas instead of bread or soda crackers. They're made something like our pancakes, but out of corn, soaked in lye water before it's ground up. They taste less like white blotting paper if you dunk one end in your plate before you bite it off."

The boy, who was named Joel, said he sure liked whatever on earth he was eating and bragged that he'd eaten tortillas before. He said there were some Mexican kids up by John Bull, even though most of the neighbors were Cousin Jacks or New Englanders like the three of them.

Longarm didn't ask why. The hardrock country was filled with the mining men from Cornwall who everyone called Cousin Jack because you could hardly hire an out-of-work tin miner from Cornwall to dig some American color for you without him saying he had a cousin named Jack back home who could drill granite with his pecker and shatter the face by farting in the bore hole.

While Longarm and the others killed time nibbling and

sipping as the noonday sun baked the rail yards outside, Longarm learned more than he figured he needed to know about the dinky mining community up at the far end of what Colorado folks called a park. In other parts they called such a flat-bottomed mountain valley a dale, a glen, or maybe a hollow.

It came as no great surprise that most of the Yankee settlers up around John Bull were farmers or stock folk. A mining camp of any size made a fair market for butter, eggs, and produce, even when you had to freight it in. Hardrock miners made three dollars a day and fed themselves and their families properly. So Flora's family had only been one of the many west-bound New Englanders who'd settled in around the silver operation poineered by that British syndicate. New England farmers were used to plowing up boulders. So they tended to accept the Rocky Mountains in a more philosophical way than some.

Flora said her bunch sold dairy produce and eggs up in John Bull, but shipped most of their barley down this way, where it commanded a way higher price. Barley didn't bake into such wondrous bread in a kitchen range. But it surely made swell beer malt. When Longarm asked if they'd heard nobody was allowed to use any other grain but barley in the Rhineland if they aimed to call it beer, young Joel proudly declared the beer brewed from John Bull barley malt was better than any High Dutch brand. Then he added that cow thieves came from all over creation to steal the swell beef they raised on the same swell mountain parklands.

Longarm didn't ask the kid to elaborate. Kids were always bragging on how tough their neighborhoods were, and cow thieves were operating everywhere you could raise cows, thanks to the recent rise in beef prices back East, now that the depression of the '70s had given way to happier paydays. So far, nobody had asked what he did for a

11

living or why he was headed the same way. So he hadn't said. Jawing about being a lawman could get tedious, even when you lied.

He introduced the three of them to tuna pie for dessert. The kids thought it was funny that you made tuna pie with red tuna cactus fruit instead of fish if you baked Mexican style. Then it was almost time to start thinking about that narrow-gauge to John Bull. So he paid up and they headed over to the loading platform, with Longarm toting the one overnight bag Flora had been hiding under her calico skirts until he'd noticed it. She kept pestering him to let her pay for their share of that *cafetín* tab. Some few gals were like that. He'd never in this world take their money, of course, but he had to admire a gal for offering.

By the time they'd made it over to the sunbaked platform, a few other fellow travelers had gotten there ahead of them. Flora knew an old lady and a young homesteading couple. So she introduced Longarm all around, and as it turned out, the old lady hadn't known the younger couple up until then, and was mighty pleased she'd be able to gossip with others instead of riding all that way with nobody to talk to.

Longarm was almost tempted to call out and include the only other passenger waiting for the narrow-gauge. It seemed a shame to leave a clean-shaven and neatly dressed young gent out. But nobody else seemed to notice the obvious stranger among them, and so Longarm hesitated to act forward as he tried to figure out why that jasper in the ready-made suit and Colorado-creased Stetson looked so familiar. The gent's commonplace face and tall lean build didn't fit any federal wants of recent urgency. But Longarm couldn't get it out of his head that the cuss reminded him of some damned body.

Then their diamond-stacked Shay locomotive puffed into

12

view with its brass bell clanging, and Longarm forgot the other man in that three-piece suit as he helped Flora and that old lady aboard. As the bunch of them were settling in aboard the one passenger car of the freight and passenger combination, Longarm heard the mysterious stranger asking the conductor what time they'd get him up to the John Bull mine.

The conductor promised they'd make it before four that afternoon. Conductors were about as honest as a cowhand dancing with a gal who was worried about her reputation. But Longarm was reassured by that lean stranger's voice. Save for the way shorter Ben Thompson, out of Yorkshire by way of Texas, there were few masters of triggernometry west of the Mississippi with British accents. So it seemed far more likely the well-dressed cuss was on some chore for the owners of the John Bull diggings. He'd spoken more London-like than your average Cousin Jack from Cornwall. So he was likely some sort of engineer. That sea chest he'd boarded with was likely loaded with his drafting tools or chemistry kit. Silver mines were trickier than most. Longarm figured they were joshing when they said you needed a gold mine to operate a silver mine, but he knew they were always having to call in some experts to tell them what in thunder they were up to down there.

The train started with a sudden jerk as if to take a run at the nine-percent grade ahead before it got to it. The results were an unexpected pleasure as the pretty Flora Munro wound up in Longarm's lap for as long as it took them to untangle, with everybody but the two of them laughing. Flora was blushing fit to bust, and Longarm felt sort of warm around the ears as she asked in vain for young Joel to trade places with her.

But big sisters didn't hold the rank it took to make a nine-year-old boy forgo a seat by the window aboard a moving train, even when the scenery outside was less interesting.

Chapter 3

As they circled Lookout Mountain the conductor got around to punching their tickets, and Longarm asked in a desperately casual tone who that other gent, now smoking out on the platform, might be. The conductor agreed he talked like a lime juicer and seemed interested in American railroading. But that was all he knew about the jasper.

Joel opined he was likely a cow thief. Flora told him to behave himself, but the barley grower across from them confirmed that there had been purloined beef up their way.

The nester, Colman by name, painted the usual picture of a few earlier and hence bigger stockmen not at all happy about that fool Homestead Act, but even more suspicious of the smaller stockmen who'd moved in on their federally owned and hence open range. Neighbors in the business of producing butter, eggs, or barley weren't as prone to increase a budding beef herd by roping with a "community loop" that included anything that looked at all like a cow.

Colman opined that the few big stockmen in the park were stewing over natural losses on rugged range, or at most, a few head stolen by the trash whites you generally found in any good-sized rural community. When Colman casually asked why Longarm was headed up to John Bull, it seemed wise for a lawman with a certain rep to answer just as casually that he wasn't in either the beef or barley business. Stealing either was a local offense. But local folks who'd lost any faith at all in a county sheriff's department were always pestering a federal deputy to hunt strays or adjudicate water rights.

He'd wired ahead he was on his way to pick up the notorious Bunny McNee, who'd been witnessed holding horses for more ferocious outlaws in the course of many a robbery, but had been arrested in John Bull for trying to sneak out of their one hotel without paying. So they wouldn't have sent him on to the county jail or turned him loose on bail before a more serious lawman could get there. But Longarm knew he'd never be able to return with the rascal before the next train back to Golden built up a morning head of steam, and he didn't want to spend the evening speculating about less important crooks.

Even Colman's mousy young wife seemed sure nobody could move any substantial number of cows out of their secluded park without anyone noticing. The lush sod grew thick and springy in what they called an intermontane climate. But once you drove anything with hooves up the wooded slopes, the thin layer of forest duff over usually soft damp sandy loam wouldn't hide the signs of your furtive drive from your average schoolmarm. So it hardly seemed likely too many cows could be all that gone. Cows were stolen to be sold for money. Nobody had any call to collect cows like stamps. But Longarm still caught himself in the act of asking whether John Bull beef was shipped out by rail or driven to market through all that pretty scenery outside.

The old lady said the railroad they were riding had helped its greedy self to the one practical right-of-way and that she and the other cow folks were mad as wet hens about that.

Colman made some soothing noises, and explained in a calmer tone how the railroad surveyors had had little choice in their route, and if anything, had shortened the original trail considerably with a cut here, a tunnel there, and more than one trestle straight across what had once been a pesky dip indeed. He said, "It hardly costs all that much more to ship beef down to the main line by narrow-gauge, if you add up the weight your cows lose on such a rugged drive. The old way was never more than a single-file trail, and the railroad's a real blessing to us barley growers. Packing barley that far to market by mule train simply ain't practical."

Longarm didn't ask why. Everyone knew pack critters had to graze for hours on free grass or be fed in far less time on grain somebody had to pay for. To pack, say, two hundred pounds of barley more than, say, sixty twisted miles, and eat as much all the way home, meant a good percentage of said barley rendered into mule shit scattered too inconveniently to gather for your rose garden. So even where farm folk moaned and groaned about rail freight charges, shipping produce more than fifty miles by rail had the dustier ways beat.

Longarm was about to inquire what this line charged by the ton when they suddenly plunged into a dark tunnel and he found it a mite more interesting to consider stealing a kiss from the perfumed temptation seated beside him.

He resisted the sudden impulse, of course. The main difference between a sensible human being and a dog was the ability to control such sudden silly notions. Then Flora was saying, "Oh, how beautiful!" as they came out the far side of the tunnel to view a wide beaver flat under a thick carpet of purple for furlongs in all directions.

Colman's wife admired the "wild lavender" as well. So Longarm and the old lady just exchanged weary glances. She was the one rude enough to say, "Lavender my foot! That's *larkspur,* and I take back what I may have said in haste about this railroad. Where on earth could all that cow-killing larkspur have come from?"

Longarm gently told her, "The old countries across the main ocean, ma'am. The old-time Greeks and Romans knew better than to let livestock graze on the pretty stuff, albeit they used it to kill lice, and you can still buy larkspur lotion at the drugstore for that. I don't know how or why larkspur wound up out *this* way. But as you can see, it surely has."

The old lady grumped, "I'd like to get my hands on the fool who planted the first Russian tumbleweed in our cow country too. Things were much nicer in these hills before thoughtless folks messed 'em up."

Longarm quietly observed some Ute and Kimoho folks he knew had said the same thing about recent changes in their Shining Mountains. Then young Joel said he knew all about larkspur lotion because he and his kid sis had been sent home from school with nits more than once.

Flora gasped and protested, "It's those white trash children from around the silver mines who keep bringing nits to school with them, the unwashed things."

The Colmans and the little old lady seemed to agree on that at least. Longarm felt sure the wives of the high-paid hardrock miners would say the kids off the surrounding farms and stock spreads were the ones in need of a bath and infested with lice. So in sum, the remote settlement of John Bull was shaping up as a typical company town surrounded by hardscrabble hill-country folk. He wasn't fixing to write a history of the place, or even mess with Flora Munro here, as tempting as she smelled. For she was a home gal as well as sort of country, and he'd told Henry he'd be back with Bunny McNee before old Billy Vail returned from that conference.

Talking about poisonous flowers had gotten the country folk into a conversation about such country matters as the local climate, like New England in the summer with the winters sort of weird. Way milder than you might expect when a sudden shift wasn't dumping as much as a dozen feet of snow between your back door and the shithouse. The high peaks all around tended to shelter the intermontane ranges from the bone-chilling wolf winds of the prairies to the east. Colorado liked to call itself the Switzerland of the West. But from what he'd read or heard from greenhorns, he figured they ought to compare it more to that Austro-Hungarian Empire, with some parts alpine while a heap of the Empire was this big prairie called an alfold, complete with cowboys who dressed sort of outlandishly.

He didn't tell his fellow travelers. He doubted they'd care, and Flora would doubtless be shocked, or think he was bragging, if he told her about himself and those immigrant sisters from Budapest. It had been the blond one who'd told him about the funny pants Hungarian cowboys wore. Folks talked about all sorts of odd things in bed as they were resting up between times.

He knew he was thinking about pillow conversations out of all proportion to the encouragement the auburn-haired Flora had given him so far. She seemed the sort of gal who expected flowers, books, and candy, along with at least a week's worth of wooing, before she gave in. And once a gal like that did, what did a man have but a heap of trouble and a limp dick on his hands? Flora Munro wasn't the sort a man could hop on and off, and even if she had been, he'd planned on no more than one night in John Bull, damn it.

He figured he'd gotten this horny by wasting that dinner

and seven acts of vaudeville on that new gal in Denver instead of a sure bet on, say, Miss Morgana Floyd of the Arvada Orphanage. Such romantic quests for novelty were always getting folks frustrated, or worse. He had to chuckle as he thought back to what a married-up pal had told him about a wild night on the town cementing his marriage.

The poor gent had been sleeping with the same wife long enough to start feeling it was a pleasant but sort of tedious chore. Then she'd had to leave town on a family emergency, and he'd found himself suddenly free to take a heap of flirty gals up on what he'd been sure they'd been offering when he couldn't take advantage of it.

But it seemed the frisky barmaid at the Black Cat already had a beau to go home with, and the shopgirl who'd been smiling at him so dewy-eyed where he went to buy his cigars had turned out to have myopia. She'd had to put her glasses back on to see who was asking her out, and as soon as she was sure it was him, she'd said not to be so silly.

And so it had gone, for a whole lot of awkward moments, as a man who'd suspected he might be a Don Juan discovered that he was only a man, and that none of the pretty gals he'd thought he was forced to pass up had ever been there for him in the first place. So by the time his wife got back, he'd had time to get horny as hell, and found her a really grand improvement on his own fist. He'd said she seemed to enjoy his hard feelings toward her as well, and that every time he'd found her a mite tedious since, he'd only had to consider how dumb it felt that other way with night coming on, your old organ-grinder hard, and no good old gal to help you out.

Longarm knew that feeling. He was fixing to face it in the near future, although he didn't get turned down often enough to do anything as desperate as proposing to gals aboard narrow-gauge combinations. Some of that reformed

Don Juan's desperation had been inspired by rusty romantic procedure. Most of the battle was in knowing who you ought to make a play for. Gents forbidden to touch tended to feel for impractical strange stuff with their imaginations. But as soon as you had all the time and freedom it took to grab for gals right, it only took a few dumb grabs to learn you only had so many turns on the old merry-go-round and it made more sense to save your time and pocket jingle for sensible targets.

Nine out of ten times the gal was the one who really determined the final results of the fandango. For while there was no way short of bribery or rape to get a gal who didn't fancy you, there was not much you could do but run like hell or take your beating like a man when she did. So Longarm usually spent more thought on ducking the dire consequences of romancing the wrong gal than he spent on getting all that romantic with anybody.

A good many miles later they commenced to see first cows and then sprawling log homes and outbuildings where a few fenced fields and lots of well-grazed but green grass sprawled across such flat parkland as there was. Longarm surmised from the way the slopes beyond had gone to aspen and lodgepole that they were now an easy timber-haul from that mining operation. You cut serious trees for mine props. Then he spied patches of logged-out lodgepole and knew they were really close. You cut lodgepole for firewood unless you were an Indian. Aspen was only good for fluttering pretty in the summer breezes.

Then, sure enough, they passed some bigger-frame structures, and slowed down as Colman explained the tracks ran on up to the mining operation after you got off at the town terminal.

That turned out to be a shingled frame structure with wide overhanging eaves, facing both the tracks and the cinder-paved town hall square. Longarm reached down for both Flora's and the old lady's carpetbags as their train hissed to a shuddering stop.

So with one awkward thing and another, Longarm and the party he was with took longer to make it down to the platform than that stranger in the suit had. Longarm spied the Englishman's heavy chest on the platform, and suspected the gent had manhandled it off on his own and then gone to fetch one or more porters. He'd just set the baggage he was carrying aside to help the two ladies down the steps when all hell commenced to bust loose in the middle distance.

Longarm yelled, "Colman, Joel, move the ladies to cover and keep 'em there whilst I find out who's shooting at whom!"

Then he was moving along the platform toward the track-side doorway of the depot with his own gun drawn, even as the echoes of that hot exchange of gunfire faded away.

He saw others crowding into the depot, and paused to break out his badge and pin it to the lapel of his own suit as his flared nostrils assured him that the depot was where that brimstone reek of spent gunpowder was drifting from. Lowering the muzzle of his .44-40 to a ready but less threatening angle, he strode on in to spy that Englishman off the train sprawled flat on his back with a puzzled smile on his face as his dead eyes stared up at the pressed-tin ceiling. A big puddle of dark red blood spread across the floorboards from the body to the baseboards of the ticket booth. Bodies drained that way when a round entered the chest from the front and blew lung tissue out the back.

Another body sprawled facedown near the far entrance. The less well-dressed badge-toting gents standing over it still had their guns out. As Longarm stepped over the big puddle of blood to call out his own connections with the law, he saw an army Schofield on the floor between the two bodies. He nodded and said, "Let me guess. That one closer to you all gunned this other jasper in direct violation of the municipal pistol ordinances, right?"

The town constable of heavier build and more substantial mustache nodded gravely and declared, "We were just outside when we heard him blasting away in here. As we tore in, there was only one man in here on his feet with a gun. I yelled at him to drop it. When that didn't seem to impress him, I fired. Now I'd like to know what in pure hell this was all about. I'd be Constable Amos Payne and this would be my deputy Nate Rothstein, by the way."

Longarm introduced himself and added, "I hope you got my earlier wire today."

Payne nodded in a distracted manner. "You can have the McNee kid any time you want. But he'd be locked up in a patent cell even as we speak, and I got me two dead bodies to account for here and now!"

Longarm reholstered his gun as he suggested, "First thing we ought to do is clear this waiting room so's we can see what we're doing. I rode up on the train with the one over yonder. He spoke with a sort of high-toned English accent. That's as much as I know about him so far."

Payne told his deputy to clear out the spectators that gunfire always seemed to attract. As he was doing so, Longarm rolled the denim-clad body on its back with a boot tip. Then he gave a soft whistle and said, "I hope the powers that be allow you to put in for bounty money, Amos."

Payne said in a puzzled tone, "It's never come up. We seldom have this much excitement here at the end of the tracks. You know who he might be, Deputy Long?"

Longarm replied, "There's no might about it. You just backshot the one and original Ginger Bancott, wanted from Texas to Nebraska for everything but spreading the whooping cough. He mostly rented his six-gun by the hour to the highest bidder. So I'd say somebody hired him to gun that more fashionable gent across the floor. You want to wire the Texas Rangers in Austin about the bounty you have coming, by the way. Big cattle baron posted a thousand on the rascal after his black sheep son got backshot by Bancott in Amarillo.''

As the two of them moved over to the other body Payne protested, ''I wish you wouldn't wrinkle your nose like that when you mention a gent getting shot in the back. I know they call you Longarm and say you're the bee's knees with your own six-gun. But I called out to the killer as he stood there with a smoking Schofield in his hand. What was I supposed to do when he didn't drop it, wait until he turned it on me?''

Longarm shook his head. ''I'd have done the same in any scene such as you've described, Amos. When I said you'd just shot a famous gunslick in the back, I never meant to imply you shouldn't have. I was only stating things as they was. An awesome amount of tedious twaddle gets printed in the papers by newspaper men who report every shooting out our way as if we were knights in armor holding sporting event at King Arthur's court.''

He dropped to one knee on the less bloody side of the dead man and reached inside the open frock coat for any possible clues as to his identity. Bancott's victim had been unarmed as well as a neater dresser. Longarm had just found an expensive pigskin billfold when a feminine voice from the far doorway called out, ''Oh, Dear Lord, that can't be Mister Gaylord Stanwyk I see there on the floor!''

Longarm suggested Deputy Rothstein let the lady in as he opened the dead man's billfold and gravely announced, ''I'm afraid it has to be, ma'am. You say you know him?''

As the Junoesque brunette of some thirty summers joined

23

them by Stanwyk's sprawled cadaver, Constable Payne introduced her as Mrs. Constance Farnsworth and added that she ran their one and only railroad. Longarm had already noticed she was wearing a fashionable black chiffon dress. So he didn't ask what her late husband might have had to do with the railroad. He rose to his more considerable height and held out the dead man's billfold to her with one hand as he ticked the brim of his Stetson to her with the other.

The vision in ebony and ivory didn't take the dead man's identification as she murmured, "We'd already met in Denver this spring. He was an established railway engineer, as the English call such gents. They lay out their railways different from our railroads and this has been a problem to us here along the John Bull Line."

Longarm gravely nodded. "I noticed the way your narrow-gauge tracks were laid, and they told me a British syndicate started the whole shebang up this way. Are we supposed to assume this poor English gent came all this way to help you run your railroad, only to be assassinated as he was getting off the train?"

The railroading widow woman agreed it certainly looked that way, but that she had no idea who'd want to do such a thing. Amos Payne allowed, and Nate Rothstein agreed, that both dead men were strangers to the small mountain community.

Longarm spied scared eyes peering at them from behind the brass bars of the one ticket window. Not wanting to step in blood, Longarm called out to ask what the old gray coot might have to add to this confusion.

The ticket clerk called back, "I saw the whole thing, but I don't know what I saw. That gent in the fancy duds had just come in off the platform, calling out something about his baggage. Next thing I knew that cuss dressed more cow over yonder had just drawn that gun on the floor and blazed away. I hit the floor on this side of my counter about the same time. Then I heard Constable Payne yell something and fire some more. I didn't feel like getting back to these tired old feet until I was sure it was all over out yonder!''

Widow Farnsworth murmured, ''Uncle Ted never lies when he's sober, and I've yet to catch him drinking on the job.''

Longarm didn't care. He felt sort of sorry for the apparently harmless Englishman. But there seemed to be no mystery as to who might have shot him. He felt curious about the motive for the killing. But whether Bancott had been hired to kill Stanwyck or simply killed a total stranger for practice, Longarm had been sent to pick up a federal want, not to solve a local tiff.

The barley-growing Colman stuck his head in the trackside entrance to yell, ''What's going on in here? Them women and children want to get off that train and . . . Hold on, ain't that gent at your feet the same one as rode up from Golden with us?''

Longarm replied, ''Yep. That other one near the far doorway did it. You can send the women and children on their way now, pard. It's all over, far as I can see.''

Longarm didn't see, of course, that his own involvement in the blood feud of John Bull had barely begun.

Chapter 4

Widow Farnsworth offered to be a sport about the body of the man she'd hired. The friendless drifter who'd gunned the railroad expert would be kept in a cool cellar for a few days and then planted over in potter's field in a newspaper shroud if nobody came forward to claim his dead meat.

By the time they'd figured all of that out it was going on supper time. But Longarm went over to the town lockup with Deputy Rothstein for a look at his own prisoner first.

The yellow sheets Longarm had read in the waiting room of Denver's Union Station had described Bunny McNee as a runty nineteen-year-old. The dirty-faced kid Rothstein called over to the bars looked far more harmless than expected. That slightly bucktoothed smirk seemed a good enough reason for the unferocious nickname.

Young McNee started to protest. "I haven't done anything deserving to be treated this mean, damn it."

Longarm quietly replied, "Nail a wreath betwixt your eyes. Your brain is dead. I'm taking you back to Denver on more serious charges than skipping out on your hotel bill, junior. But there's no train we can catch before tomorrow morning. So another night in that box won't hurt you, and meanwhile, I want you to study some on the fatherly advice I'm about to give you."

Bunny McNee asked if he could have some tobacco, or at least some soap to wash up with.

Longarm said, "I might leave you with a couple of cheroots, and I reckon I could manage a cake of soap early enough in the morning for you to clean up for that train ride if I wanted to. They tell me you've been carrying on like a spoiled brat instead of a grown man who knows he's done wrong. So the question for you to help me decide is whether I want to. I don't *have* to give you any breaks at all. I can slap you in cuffs and leg irons and let you ride in the baggage car, or we can head back to Denver like a sensible sinner and a man just doing his job."

McNee said, "I follow your drift and I don't mean to give you any trouble, Longarm."

The tall lawman reached under his coat for some smokes as he said, "That's not the main advice I'd like you to sleep on, kid. I'm taking you to talk about shoes and ships and sealing wax with Judge Dickerson of the Denver District Court. You'll find him firm but fair. He won't take shit off anyone who's ever bent the law. But on the other hand, the only charges that'll stick to you for certain are aiding and abetting. You've for sure been aiding and abetting the sort of friends your mama warned you against. So the judge is sure to be more interested in them than the kid seen holding the horses and such."

He passed out cheroots for the three of them and handed the kid a fourth one through the bars, even as McNee protested, "They *are* my friends, dad blast it! Do I look like the sort who'd peach on a pal just to butter up some old judge?"

You caught more flies with honey than with vinegar. So Longarm managed not to say the prisoner looked a lot like exactly that as he thumbed a match head aflame to light all their smokes. "I have heard of that code of silence. Seen it in one of Buntline's Wild West magazines too. So it must be true. What I'd like you to ponder, in the wee small hours you have left thanks to the narrow-gauge timetable, is the year or more of hard labor Judge Dickerson *could* throw at you against your walking out of the Denver Federal Building with me for a friendly drink at the nearby Parthenon Saloon before we each went our separate ways on a soft summer night."

McNee gasped, "I couldn't! They'd track me down no matter where I ran to!"

To which Longarm replied with an annoyed snort of smoke, "Not if you helped us round the whole bunch up. Even if we missed a few, there'd be nothing about your peaching on them in the court records. We only need some names and addresses, kid. You don't have to sign a single warrant with your own name."

The young owlhoot rider didn't answer. So Longarm nodded soberly and said, "You take your time and think it over. It's no skin off my ass if you'd rather make little rocks out of biggers ones for the sake of your swell pals."

He enjoyed another drag on his own cheroot and added, "We have a whole night ahead of us. I'm fixing to bed down in that same hotel you were charged with sneaking out of. I aim to pay them for their services to me. I'm surprised you were caught creeping out like an abandoned woman, seeing your outlaw pals are so loyal to one another."

Bunny McNee flushed mighty red, but still refused to answer. Longarm chuckled fondly and told the town lawman, "We'd best let him jerk off in private over his true blue asshole amigos. Anyone can see they've left him to face the music alone, right?"

Rothstein was an experienced lawman as well. So as the two of them strode away the town lawman replied, as if for Longarm's ears alone, "That's for damned sure. Any real pal with the price of a few beers could have bailed him out on that theft-of-service charge before we had any notion he was wanted by you boys."

As they got out front, Rothstein asked if Longarm thought it was going to work.

Longarm shrugged and said, "Depends on whether the kid got into that fix on his own or with some help. From the little we know about the gang he's been riding with, they divvy the take and split up after each robbery. McNee might have blown his own share a dozen different ways as he was laying low up here. I mean to ask around, if I have the time."

Rothstein said, "We already did. The kid never blew that much on cards or the few whores left in town now that the silver lode has about bottomed out."

Longarm whistled softly. "Heard things had started to slow down up this way. Hadn't heard they were *that* slow. Usual story with Front Range silver carbonate? The high-grade setting on top of base metal like icing on a cake?"

Rothstein shrugged. "I don't know enough about mining to argue. The way I heard it, they keep smelting more and more lead and zinc out of the crushed rock by the time they run it all the way to the smelters on the main line. So the British syndicate's had to sell things off, a holding at a time, to keep things going at all."

Longarm nodded absently and muttered, "That accounts for the railroad being run by a widow gal of our own persuasion. Our Bunny McNee likely figured a town withering on the vine was a better place to lay low than either a boom town or an outright ghost town where a stranger would stand out even more."

Rothstein said, "I follow your drift. We had him down as no more than a drifter who'd failed to get hired up at the mine and run out of eating money before yours truly got to killing time with some old wanted fliers. Amos says he figures that gang splits up between robberies and then gets together for another after things cool down from the last one."

By this time they were out on the walk. The sky above had turned dusky rose, the peaks to the east to flame, the peaks to the west deep purple, and everything between sort of murky lavender. So Longarm said, "I was wondering why I was getting so hungry. Constable Amos Payne and my boss, Marshal Billy Vail, think a heap alike. McNee has to know where his pals are fixing to get together again, and you just now heard me tell him why he ought to confide in us. By the time I have him in Judge Dickerson's chambers tomorrow afternoon, he ought to be willing to explain all the details for us. I was fixing to bed down in that same Elk Rack Hotel he snuck out of. Might that be as wise a move as it sounds?"

Rothstein allowed the Elk Rack was as good a hotel as he'd ever find in John Bull, being it was the only one. So they shook on it and parted friendly in the tricky light of a mountain gloaming.

As Longarm headed up the plank walk in the deep shade of the overhanging snowsheds, a few of the establishments he passed were lit up. But most had either closed for the night or for good, with their windows boarded over or shabby pasteboard signs in grimy windows wistfully promising a glowing future at a great location for anyone who wanted to rent or, hell, buy the property outright cheap.

As he passed the swinging doors of a lamp-lit hole-in-the-wall saloon, a rinky piano burst into life. Longarm paused in mid-stride to peer in. Then he started walking again and, sure enough, so did that pair of high-heeled Justins that had come to a clunking halt when his army boots had just now.

That was more interesting to Longarm than the identity of the awful piano player inside. A quick glance at a flash of bright red had confirmed his suspicion there was only one person in these parts who could make a living playing piano in the cracks between the keys. So now that he knew where Miss Red Robin was working here in John Bull, he wanted to know who was following him and how come.

He strode on toward the one hotel, trying to act neither hurried nor suspicious until he got to the next corner, ducked around it, and backed into the shade of some side stairs as he clunked in place to sound as if he was still going.

It worked. Those high-heeled boots came around the corner on the double as Longarm tried for the sound of boot heels fading away in the distance. So then it was a simple matter of reaching out to grab a fistful of shirt, swinging the cuss around to slam into the painted pine siding, and shoving a gun muzzle in his face for him to smell as its owner growled, "You've caught up with me at last, you sly son of a bitch. And now you're fixing to tell me what you had in mind if you'd like your brains to remain in your skull this evening."

What appeared a cowhand at Longarm's mercy gulped hard and asked if this might be a robbery.

Longarm didn't need to cock his double action .44-40, but he'd found in the past that snicking back the hammer seemed to underscore the message. So he snicked it as he bounced the young hand against the wall, saying, "*I'm* the one demanding some damned *answers* here, and when I implied your brains might be blown out this evening, I never meant *later* this evening. You've been walking in

31

step with me two full blocks and around that corner. I ain't going to ask you again why you did so.''

The younger but sizeable local, who didn't seem to be packing a gun of his own on either denim-clad hip, gulped hard and decided to say, ''You ain't allowed to shoot me fatal for no reason, lawman!''

So Longarm sighed and said, ''That's true. I have to put some halfway sensible reason on my official report when I gun one of you assholes. But seeing you know who *I* am, asshole, you ought to know I can write official as hell, and here we are, with darkness falling, nary a witness in sight, and you following me from a jail where I just now questioned a dangerous criminal. Your turn, asshole.''

His victim blanched and protested, ''See here, I had nothing to do with the killing of that lime juicer this afternoon, and I've never in this world laid eyes on that outlaw Amos Payne was holding for you all.''

Longarm made a mental note that the mysterious cuss knew the local law by name. Anyone who'd just come to town could have heard about the killing at the railroad depot a good four hours back. Longarm said, ''In that case you'd better tell me what you *have* been up to.''

The kid said, ''All right. I don't want you messing with my Flora in any damned case. When I heard about her sparking with a big lawman from Denver aboard the train from Golden this afternoon, I had every right in this world to confront her about it. So I did. After a gal I've come calling on more than once told me I was a moon calf she didn't want to visit with no more, I had every right in this world to suspect it was yourself she meant to be visiting with this evening. So I've been watching you, meaning to pop outten the shadows and call Flora Munro something worse than a moon calf when and if my suspicions panned out correct!''

Longarm laughed wearily and let go of the front of the lovesick cowhand's shirt. "She had no call to imply your were a moon calf when anyone can see you're a total asshole. I don't even know where your Flora and her kid brother and sister live. I got to talking with the bunch of them as we were waiting for that train together. On the way up the narrow-gauge line I talked as much to two other ladies and I sure hope nobody suspects me of sparking with *them*!"

He put his pistol away as he added, "Since this means so much to you, I was headed for the Elk Rack Hotel to hire a room for the night. After that I mean to enjoy me a sit-down supper and I may or may not seek further adventure with an old pal of the female persuasion. You have my word as a man I ain't aiming to mess with any home gal you've been courting, and come morning I'll be leaving town with my prisoner in any case. So do we have peace or war here?"

The big dumb kid said he reckoned he could have been mistaken.

Longarm nodded and said, "That's good enough for me. You know who I am. So who might *you* be, amigo?"

The kid muttered, "I'd be Will Posner, off the Lazy Three, but I don't see as it matters, seeing you're leaving town with honorable intentions towards my Flora Munro."

To which Longarm grimly answered, "It won't matter to either of us unless I catch you trailing me through the gathering darkness again. I'm buying your story this time. You're going to have more trouble selling your innocent foolishness a second time, and like you said, they expect official reports, with as many names as possible."

Chapter 5

Summer nights were cool at that altitude. So Longarm hired a one-window room facing away from the street and then, with his hotel key in a side pocket, had a late supper downstairs. It was just as well he sat down to the table hungry as a bitch wolf. For while the spuds were fair and the peas were doubtless good for him, the meat they'd advertised as elk steak, ordered rare, seemed to have been left over from that elk rack the hotel was named after.

But he cut it fine and ate it all, reflecting on how the poor Ute and Kimoho had fought so hard to hang on to their elk-infested high country where the buffalo had seldom roamed.

Thinking about buffalo could make a man feel wistful as he gnawed on elk meat. But, of course, in their Shining Times the Indians had selectively shot does and fawns instead of magnificent stags for the pot. Lakota were about the only Indians in these parts who seemed to give a hoot about the skulls of bigger buffalo bulls, and even they preferred fat cows and calves for eating.

Reflecting on how the mummified elk remains he'd just swallowed would stick with him and blot up beer all evening, Longarm shoved his chair back from the table and called the lonesome-looking waitress to his side. She looked lonesome because at that hour there was nobody else to be seen under the log-beamed ceiling of the cavernous hotel dining room. When she nervously asked him what was wrong, he suspected other guests with weaker jaws had commented on a noble stag who'd been allowed to die of old age before they carved his carcass up.

He gently said, "There's nothing wrong, ma'am. I generally eat till I've had enough and then I stop. I had some tuna pie earlier today, and I can still taste the sorghum sugar. So I reckon I'd as soon pass on them desserts you got on your menu. But you can fetch me another cup of black coffee if you like."

She did, saying, "You must be that lawman from Denver." As she refilled his mug, she added, "They said someone was coming to get that snotty kid who tried to leave town without paying all his just debts. How come they call you Longarm? I'll allow you're tall, but your arms don't look unnatural to me, no offense."

He chuckled and explained. "My last name's Long. I mean I'd be Custis Long, not that my handle is protracted. Some reporter seems to have put that together with the way I'm sometimes sent to act as the long arm of the law and decided I was Longarm. But you can call me Custis, ma'am."

She dimpled and replied, "In that case you can call me Matilda Waller, out of York State by way of some misspent years in Kansas, and I get off work here at midnight."

Longarm sipped some coffee before he said, "I know the feeling. I would rather work most any shift but noon to midnight no matter what my job was. You say that outlaw Bunny McNee was snotty to you?"

She wrinkled her nose and replied, "He never got *fresh*

with me, or left a tip for anybody during his stay here. Peony, the chambermaid, told us he was one of those sissy boys who didn't like girls."

Longarm took another sip and asked, "Do tell? How did Miss Peony come to this conclusion? Did Bunny McNee tell her he didn't like her?"

The waitress laughed and said, "Not many men pester poor Peony that way. I've *told* her to cut down on sweets, but she says she needs the energy. She says she was working upstairs when she got to Mr. McNee's Don't Disturb sign and heard all this moaning and groaning coming from inside, as if he wasn't alone in bed after all."

Longarm swallowed a little distaste with some coffee as well. Such petty gossip would have been none of his beeswax if Bunny McNee had been simply a fellow guest at a hotel with a nosy staff. But they'd sent him all this way in *search* of gossip along the owlhoot trail. So he suggested, "Young squirts have been known to moan and groan alone in bed, being broke in a strange town with nobody to talk to save for a friendly hand."

The waitress grinned like a mean little kid and warned him such habits would grow hair on one's palms. Then she confided, "He wasn't playing with himself. Peony was watching, from another room, when another young rider she'd never seen before slipped out, grinning to himself like a dirty dog. Peony allowed he was more manly-looking and should have been able to get a real girl. But that's the way some men seem to behave, the silly things."

Longarm had about finished his second coffee. He asked if anyone had seen that other stranger since.

Matilda shook her head and replied, "That sissy deadbeat was all alone when they caught him just outside of town. They never expected to. For he'd already hopped the narrow-gauge to Golden by the time the manager discovered he'd skipped out on his bill. But the train got stopped by fallen rocks across the track and had to back up all the way home. So Constable Payne's boys were waiting for him at the station. How come they sent a federal deputy all this way after a sissy who tried to cheat this hotel?''

Longarm murmured there was a mite more to it than that. Then he left a dime near his empty plate, knowing three meals a day would be covered by his American plan hotel bill, and mosied out to see what Red Robin might have to say for herself.

Red Robin was what they called a mighty pretty piano player with one hell of a figure and no musical talent worth mentioning. Longarm had met her down Texas way a spell back, when she'd fortunately been on the run after gunning a son of a bitch who'd deserved it to begin with and hadn't really died in the end.

As Longarm parted the batwing doors of the saloon she was playing in that evening, he had to wince as he suddenly realized Red Robin was groping across the keys for the tune of "Lorena" when he'd been assuming she was trying to play "Aura Lee." He liked the surprises she sprang pounding bedsprings better. But he found himself a place at the bar and quietly ordered a scuttle of draft to sip while she finished a set. It sounded dreadful when Red Robin was really startled at the piano.

As he sipped, he viewed her lovely rear view with an anticipation of more intimate views to follow. Red Robin liked it dog-style, and the best part was that she never made a pal feel guilty in the wan gray light of dawn. For like himself, Red Robin led a tumbleweed life that called for grabbing such prudent pleasures as fate offered and never holding others to promises too awkward to keep.

From her scarlet velveteen dress and matching upswept hair, one gathered Red Robin admired red. Longarm sus-

pected she might be a natural brunette, but he wouldn't
have bet big money on this because she shaved under her
arms and between her creamy thighs. She said a gal who
lived on the road had to watch out for bugs. That might
have been why she wore no unmentionables under that
tight-bodiced scarlet dress. Her skirts were long enough to
keep such secrets, and pals who knew her as well as Longarm never told.

He had a pretty good erection for the pretty little thing
by the time Red Robin stopped in what seemed like mid-
stream and got up to see if anyone clapped. Some of the
boys did, as soon as they figured out what she was doing.
Everyone of the male persuasion liked Red Robin to *look*
at, and when she was just smiling so pretty, nobody had to
listen.

Longarm had expected Red Robin to look surprised as
their eyes met through the tobacco haze. But he didn't
know what to make of her odd expression as she gulped
and waved at a corner table for the two of them.

They each made their separate ways there, with more
customers asking her to marry them, and sat down across
from one another. He knew a lady of around thirty had no
call to drink beer between meals, and no professional en-
tertainer with a lick of sense drank the hard stuff. But he
still felt obliged to ask her if she wanted him to order something for her.

Red Robin shook her head, licked her painted lips, and
murmured, "I heard you were in town. They said you'd
only be here overnight."

Longarm left his own beer untasted as he nodded. "They
told you true. But the night is young and I got a swell room
over to the Elk Rack Hotel, honey."

She looked down at the table and replied, "Me too. I've
been staying there myself. This will be my last night here

38

in John Bull. Things have gotten slow and I hear there's way more action at that new camp, Holy Cross, on the other side of the Divide.''

Longarm grinned as if he'd just been dealt a face card and told her, ''There is. I was just over yonder a spell back. But to get to Holy Cross from here you have to take the trains on back to Denver, transfer to the Leadville Line, and then . . .''

''Custis, I'm heading over the mountains the shorter way, by mule train, with . . . company come morning.''

To which Longarm could only reply, ''Oh. In that case we'll say no more about tonight.''

She placed her cool hand atop his left wrist and quietly explained, ''It's not as if I was expecting *you* to show up here, Custis.''

He smiled gamely, and said, ''Hell, if you hadn't been in town I would have gone after somebody else and we both know it. I thought we'd agreed on some rules that night in that army tent up betwixt Ward and Jimtown.''

She almost sobbed. ''I know we promised never to make any promises. Even though you'd just made me come again, you reasonable cuss. It's just that I never want to hurt you and yet . . .''

''You've been offered a ride over the Divide by some other gent going your way.'' He turned his hand over to take hers as he said soothingly, ''It's going to work out fine, pretty lady. I was just now telling a love-struck swain what a fool he looked for pestering a stranger who'd meant him no harm over a similar situation. I don't aim to stay here and glower at this other gent you've decided to go riding with of your own free will.''

He took a last sip of suds, set the scuttle aside, and continued with a wistful smile. ''I ain't up to one of them stiff-upper-lipping drawing room scenes neither. So I reckon I'd best get it on up the road.''

Red Robin smiled back uncertainly and said, ''The least you could do for my self-confidence would be to make a counteroffer, Custis!''

He rose from the table and soberly assured her, ''I would if I could. But I'm headed for Denver with a prisoner in the morning, whilst you're headed for Holy Cross with somebody else. So let's say no more about it, hear?''

He turned and strode off through the blue haze without looking back. Some kindly philosopher had once written, doubtless in French, that there was nothing a rejected lover could say to a woman dealing the cards that topped a polite farewell. For the only sight sillier than a cuss with a red face was a *cussing* cuss with a red face, and graceful losers unsettled women more.

He barely made it to the corner outside before he heard the gal who'd rejected him pounding harder and worse than ever on the piano. He chuckled, lit a fresh cheroot, and kept walking. The evening was young but the opportunities in a town this size seemed limited. So it made more sense to buy something to read, turn in early, and get back to Denver and the main action all rested up for some action.

He stopped at a corner shop near his hotel to stock up on more smokes and the latest issue of *Scientific American*. He'd found in the past that trying to keep up with all those newfangled notions tended to either educate a man or put him to sleep earlier. He had no call to stop at the desk as he entered the Elk Rack. He'd stayed in enough hotels to know the educated way to manage one's room key was to hang on to it until you were fixing to leave and either turn it in at the desk or leave it on the bed if there was a catch lock you could shut behind you as you and the lady used the discreet back stairs. Hotels only got sore when you left without paying up.

So Longarm was mildly surprised when the elderly room clerk hailed him from behind the desk. But as he strode over politely to explain he had his key in his pocket, the clerk said an errand boy had left a message for him.

The scented envelope the hotel man handed over was the color of old ivory. It seemed a shame to tear open such expensive paper, but he had to if he wanted to read what was inside. So he did.

It was from that handsome Widow Farnsworth, although she'd signed it Constance. She allowed she wanted to talk to him about a matter of grave importance and that she'd be receiving until ten that evening. So it had to be important indeed. Most invitations were for no later than eight.

He consulted his pocket watch, saw he had close to an hour, and went on up to toss that magazine on the bed and make sure he didn't need a shave before he went back down and headed up the slope to the address included in the invitation.

It wasn't far. Nothing was all that far in a town the size of John Bull, but as was only to be expected, the mustard-yellow and mansard-roofed Farnsworth mansion was well uphill and windward of the railroad yards, stockyards, municipal corral, and such.

A stuffy colored butler, who made Longarm think of a frog dipped in chocolate and dressed up like the late Prince Albert, opened the big front door and insisted on taking Longarm's hat away from him. Then he ushered him into the parlor, where Constance Farnsworth lounged on a satin sofa in a summer-weight dress the same ivory shade as her fancy writing paper. It sure set her jet-black hair and lavender eyes off in a flattering way. He noticed the drapery and matching satin of the sofa were the exact same color

41

as her eyes. A lady had to have money to decorate her house like that.

She rose all the way to greet him, like a real sport, and told him refreshments were on the way. So they both sat down on opposite ends of that sofa with their knees behind a low-slung rosewood table. Sure enough, a white gal dressed in French maid's livery soon came in to set down a tea tray heaped with a sterling silver service and more vittles than you'd think such a dainty little thing could carry.

Longarm was game for tea, no cream or sugar, and he knew he was supposed to let Constance Farnsworth pour and reach for that fancy pastry first. So he just sat tight and as she served them both, the widow woman quietly told him, "I've been thinking about the murder of Gaylord Stanwyk. I told you why I'd sent for him."

Longarm nodded soberly. "Heard about them rockslides you have from time to time along your tracks. I reckon I'd send away for a civil engineer if I was having trouble with running a railroad through these mountains too, ma'am."

She'd finished pouring and picked up her cup, meaning he was free to do the same, as she said, "Like the tracks up the slope to that British mining operation, the narrow-gauge line to the outside world was built by engineers trained in England, using the rails and other hardware they were accustomed to."

Longarm picked up a macaroon, but didn't bite into it before he told her, "I'd already noticed your rolling stock and sort of fancy tracks, ma'am. You'd hired Stanwyk to do some repairs on it for you because he knew how to work with it?"

She shook her head and said, "Not exactly. You're so right about the line being overdue for some heavy repairs. Between the heavy ore loads and rocks that simply seems

42

to fall on the track from the sky in this crazy Colorado weather, we've been running once a day each way at slower speeds than our customers approve of."

Longarm had already noticed that coming up from Golden. So he just bit into the macaroon and sipped some tea as she went on about meeting up with that British railroad man in Denver and him telling her he could get her trains to running right again cheap.

When she got to the part about somebody hiring the late Ginger Bancott to gun her engineer before he could even take a gander at her beat-up tracks, Longarm cut in to say, "Hold on, Miss Constance. I follow your drift, and it's already occurred to both Constable Amos Payne and myself that somebody with some motive must have paid that otherwise useless gun waddie to lay for your engineer like that. But even if you could give me some names and addresses, I'd still be the same federal lawman with no federal jurisdiction up here as far as I can see. Bancott shot a man dead in your local depot and got shot in return by your local law, making it a local matter for your local coroner's jury to record and file. I don't see how anybody could stand trial in any court, local, state, or federal, on our mere suspicion of ulterior motives."

She looked so let down by such common sense that, even though he knew better, he found himself saying, "All right. Who do you suspect of ordering your repair man murdered?"

She messed it up by answering in a reasonable tone, "I can't be certain. But I've had more than one offer to take the line off my delicate female hands cheap."

He quietly said he'd locked horns with such helpful gents in his time.

She said, "I know. I read about you dealing with that cabal trying to rob that young heiress. It was in both the

Denver Post and *Rocky Mountain News*. That's why I sent for you.''

He was too polite to remark that she hadn't struck him as a young heiress. But as if she'd read his mind, she continued, ''In this case it was my late husband who took over the narrow-gauge and some other local businesses as the original British syndicate found that silver operation ever less profitable and began to sell their local holdings off. I'll admit it hardly seems anyone murdered him, the way that big Texas rancher was murdered by his business rivals in that case I just mentioned. My poor Claude simply died young, two years ago this summer, from working his poor heart too hard at this altitude. But after that, all my troubles seem a lot like those of that younger and doubtless prettier businesswoman!''

He assured her, ''Looks had nothing to do with it, ma'am. The case to which you refer was federal because an interstate as well as ruthless bunch of killers was trying to horn in on a business empire that was far more widespread than Texas and doing business with the U.S. Government besides. No offense, but might you be carrying passengers or freight for, say, the army or an Indian agency across a state line?''

To which she could only reply with a gallant defeated smile that they both knew that Indian-fighting and all the poor Ute Indians were fading memories along the Front Range.

By this time Longarm had bitten into a chocolate-stuffed napoleon even better than her macaroons. So he agreed he'd at least hear a lady out. But it was good thing her pastries were fresh, because her sad story wasn't.

Longarm had read about why the nonferrous ores of the Rockies had settled out of solution much the same no matter where you built a boom town, but he hadn't retained

44

the details. Prospectors tended to pan loose placer gold in modest amounts from Colorado creeks, follow the color upstream to the mother lodes the nuggets and dust were washing out of, and dig through a crust of gold into silver with a little lead into ever-increasing amounts of lead.

It was at this point that hardrock mining turned from easy money to a serious industry, with the mine owners having to decide whether to go into the lead-extraction business at modest profit after a heap of retooling, or just pack it in and go find some high-grade somewhere else.

Many a recently booming mining camp had turned almost overnight to a ghost town, abandoned to the lonesome winds because it cost more to haul lumber and hardware to such a remote neck of the woods than it did to start fresh in other parts, paying for the more expensive hauling one single way.

Where bottomed-out lodes had been struck near more sensible townsites, their towns tended to hang on under new management. Denver had been the pre-war gold camp of Cherry Creek. Now it was the capital of Colorado without a speck of color to be panned for in that sandy old creek near Longarm's hired quarters, save for hopeful kids from that brownstone school over on Lincoln Street.

Leadville was still going strong, and even growing, after changing its ways to smelt low-grade in bulk, while Golden was holding on as its gold ran low in a manner Constance Farnsworth recommended as the salvation of John Bull.

Longarm had to agree the town outside was nestled at the high end of a fertile mountain park with the surrounding slopes still fairly well timbered and, for all they knew, still infested with color nobody had prospected yet. Lots of housing and business structures still stood with their paint nearly fresh, and anyone could see how many folks there still were for the business district and railroad to serve.

When he finished a small jelly roll and said he'd just talked to a piano player getting ready to pull stakes and move on to another boom, the widow woman curled her kissable upper lip and said her town would be better off without the usual boom-town crowd. She pointed out—and he had to agree—that the gunslick he'd been sent to transfer back to Denver never might have tried to lie low in this part of the high country if he hadn't been misled to believe it was still booming full blast.

Longarm smiled thinly and dryly replied that still meant three or more folks who were staying that night in John Bull would be long gone before the sun ever set again.

Then he relented and said, "Sorry, ma'am, that was aiming at an easy target with ten-gauge birdshot. I've met up with folks raising beef and barley up your way, and I know for a fact they'll have to use your railroad if they mean to stay. It's starting to sound like that joke about a town where everyone gets by by taking in one another's laundry, but let's buy the notion for now and get to why someone seems out to steal your profitable little railroad."

She sighed and said, "You're so right about it being little, and the profits are barely enough to keep it going. I've only kept the line running because it serves my more profitable enterprises here at this end of the park and, well . . . out of respect for a dreamer who literally worked his heart to an early grave in better times."

He washed down another napoleon, allowed her sentiments did her late husband proud, and asked her what her other enterprises might be.

They turned out to be cattle, barley, a lumber yard, and a hardware store. He whistled and said he saw why she needed a railroad. She told him the same people who'd bought out the British silver mine and aimed to smelt lead ingots on their site had offered to buy her railroad as well.

So despite knowing better, he had to dig deeper by saying, "Some business tycoons would sell their mother's false teeth the day she dies and had no profitable use for 'em. But that leaves others such as the lamp oil king, John D. Rockefeller, who'd rather buy out everyone they do business with. So, no offense, gents offering a lady good money for her railroad don't have to be up to anything more sinister than pure greed."

She grimaced and replied, "I'd be perfectly willing to sell out for *good* money. They've offered a tenth what Claude and I paid when we bought it from investors anxious to divest themselves of American holdings."

He didn't answer. His mouth was full. He just listened as she continued. "Rail fares and other investments we made up this way have paid off the bank loans and left me moderately well off, as you can see. I don't mean to leave all we built here unless selling out would leave me stinking rich. But when I told those mean people that, they said they'd just wait until my railroad went broke and buy it off the bankruptcy court clerk even cheaper!"

Longarm whistled and said, "That *does* sound mean, and patient as a beaver trapper besides. Ain't you likely to keep your narrow-gauge going indefinitely, in its own pokey way, no offense?"

She sighed and said, "Not without some serious track maintenance. It keeps getting worse as my few track workers make jury-rig repairs on breaks that are often suspicious along close to eighty miles of curves. I can't lay new trackage with the Stevens pattern rails I can afford in sensible amounts. I have to replace rail that's banged up or dangerously worn down with that heavier and more expensive Wilkinson rail from England, when I can *get* it. None of the other lines this far west have any on hand, even as scrap. The oily new mine owners have offered to sell me some of the replacement stock left by that original British syndicate, at about the price for sterling silver. Before they had him killed this morning, Gaylord Stanwyk was going to show me how to get around the stranglehold. Down in Denver he assured me he might have a simple solution, once he surveyed just what Claude and I had bought up here in the first place.''

Longarm put down his empty cup and gravely said, ''A railroad who learned his craft in England would have doubtless known way more about fancy English railroad tracks. Have you considered just converting the whole line to far cheaper American rails, speaking of solutions?''

She shook her brunette head and replied, ''It's not that cheap when you're talking about tearing out and replacing *that* much track. It was naturally the first thought I had, when my maintenance crews first told me we were running low on replacement stock. I had an *American* civil engineer run an estimate for me. I'd come out ahead if I sold my line to those mean people at their price.''

Longarm started to reach for his notebook. Then he reflected there could be no secret as to who might own and operate the only mining operation for miles. Besides he'd never been sent up this way to investigate that. So he politely covered his empty cup with a palm before she could pour more. Then he told her, ''When I get back to Denver I can lay your business worries before a firm but fair old cuss I know on the state railroad commission. But I fear nothing you've been able to tell me sounds at all federal and, no offense, I was aiming on an early start in the morning with my prisoner. I got to get him up, feed him, and process some infernal paperwork long before your morning train heads down to Golden.''

She rose with him, placing a hand on one sleeve as she insisted she stood ready to make it worth his while if he'd like to work for her as well as the government.

He wasn't sure just how she meant that, and he was still hurting from Red Robin's unexpected change in his plans. But he still told her, "I'll be seeing that railroad commissioner for you on my own time, ma'am. That's about the best I can offer. My boss, Marshal Vail, frowns on his deputies renting their guns by the hour on the side."

She gasped. "Good heavens! Nobody said anything about hiring you as a gunfighter, Custis!"

To which he could only reply, "That's what it boils down to as I consider your tale, ma'am. You offer no evidence a lawman could use to make any arrests. We both know I ain't a Civil engineer. What's left after that but gunning your rivals for you?"

She protested she'd had no such thing in mind. So he didn't press her. He left her stewing there and ambled off to find that butler and get his hat back.

As he was doing so, the pretty but hard-eyed maid who'd served him and her mistress in the parlor was out back in the darkness with a gent in the business Longarm had just said his boss disapproved of.

The maid repeated that she'd been able to hear every word from her position just outside an open doorway. But the gunslick and occasional lover who'd stationed her there wanted her to assure him some more.

She said, "I told you, hon. Miss Constance tried to recruit him as her own Pinkerton man and he kept saying no. He really *did* come up our way just to carry that prisoner in the jail back to Denver."

Her late night caller shrugged and replied, "I'll be back to tell you exactly want I want from you after I report to the powers that be about that keen-edged lawman. They'll likely be inclined to agree with you if he gets aboard that

49

morning train with the McNee kid.''

Then he said, ''We'll know he was *on* to you, or playing some sneaky lone hand, should he fail to catch that morning train out of here!''

Chapter 6

Longarm got back to his hotel at a hellishly awkward hour. It was way too late to meet up with any dance-hall gals who hadn't already met somebody else if they had one head and two legs. But it was way too early for that friendly waitress, Matilda, to be getting off.

Hotel people tended to work staggered shifts, from, say, nine in the morning to nine at night or, like poor Matilda, from noon to midnight. He didn't peek in as he passed the archway leading into their dining room as he crossed the lobby once more. He could hear enough clinking and jawing to tell business was picking up again in there. Gents who ate early suppers so they could go out and paint the town tended to console themselves with late snacks before they gave up and went to bed alone. Longarm knew the feeling, but thanks to all that fancy pastry up the slope just now, he doubted he could get down so much as a bowl of chili.

He climbed the stairs, hauling out his key on the rise, and made sure nobody had been inside in his absence. That only called for a suspicious nature and a match stem wedged in the bottom door hinge as you locked up.

Inside, he struck a fresh match to light the bed lamp, shot the bolt as he shut the door, and peeled down to the buff before he got in bed with his magazine and a fresh cheroot. He read that that one-armed explorer, John Wesley Powell, was trying to start up a U.S. Geological Survey, run by the government, to figure things out more sensibly out this way.

As a lawman, Longarm had to agree a heap of folks had managed to get killed fighting over fool's gold or range that wouldn't support a really hungry rabbit. Old Powell was for irrigating the best parts and leaving most of it the hell alone.

Then there was yet another plan to build horseless carriages or rubber-tired locomotives that didn't need tracks. Longarm could have told the poor inventor why his invention wasn't going to work. Anyone who knew how to make a steam engine could see how to set a small one on a wagon, hooked up to the wheels instead of steamboat paddles. A Frenchman had built himself a three-wheeled horseless carriage back before their revolution, scared folks half to death, and damned near gotten himself killed when he ran off the road and through a stone wall.

Railroaders didn't lay all that expensive trackage just to expend the time and money. Tracks smoothed out the bumps and steered such a sudden and heavy mass of machinery the right way. Nobody was likely to get anywhere with self-propelled vehicles before the roads got a whole lot smoother or those rubber tires got a whole lot softer than anyone knew how to build them yet.

Suddenly aware the dumb article was having the desired effect on his eyelids, Longarm got rid of the smoke before he could set himself and the whole hotel on fire. Then he tossed the magazine aside and trimmed the lamp, muttering, ''That pretty widow would have no problem if only she could buy a cross-country steam tractor strong enough to haul, say, a string of sledges the length of that whole park in summer weather. But she can't. So we'll say no more about it.''

He plumped up his two pillows and flopped his head down on them to shut his eyes and try not to think of pretty gals in either red velveteen or ivory damask sheathing shapely derrieres. He and his dawning erection would have settled for a dishwater blonde in that cotton waitress uniform about now. So he idly wondered if he might have room for just a cup of coffee downstairs.

He muttered half aloud in the dark, ''It's barely ten o'clock, you poor hard-up simp, and even after she gets off at midnight you'd have to spend an hour or more getting her up here and into this blamed bed. So simmer down and let's get a fresh start in the morning and, with any luck, that court stenographer called Bubbles will be willing to enjoy another noon break with you in that file room.''

Thinking about something else tended to help a poor cuss with a hard-on in a strange town. So Longarm pondered some more about the way Englishmen and Chinamen laid railroad track. He'd read a book on the subject one time, if only he could recall the title. It had given the advantages and disadvantages of either system. But all he managed to remember was that those heavier English rails cost far more money and took far more work to set securely in place. He'd already agreed with young Widow Farnsworth about that.

As he lay there in the dark, picturing cross sections of the two kinds of track in his mind's eye, someone seemed to be gently tapping on his chamber door. He doubted like hell it could be a raven, and Matilda Waller was still on duty down below. So Longarm tossed his covers aside and rolled to his bare feet with a full erection and a knowing grin. For Red Robin had seen him like this in broad daylight and he could hardly wait to hear her explanation—after they'd torn some off, of course. If she still meant to ride off across the Divide with some other son of a bitch, he didn't want to hear about it while he was coming in her fickle flesh.

That thought had Longarm a mite miffed as he flung open the door of his dark room to the dark hallway and simply grabbed hold to haul the surprised gal in, muttering, "Great minds seem to run in the same channels. I was fixing to start without you, but seeing you're in as horny a mood, let's ride her to Powder River and see how she bucks!"

"Not so loud!" his late-night female visitor whispered as he simply swept her off her feet and headed for the bed with her skirts brushing against his bare legs. He'd noticed back in that saloon how Red Robin's large rump had spread across a piano stool a mite more since last he'd had her dog-style. But it wasn't polite to warn any gal she was getting fat. So he never did as he flopped her across his rumpled bedding and hoisted her skirts high without further ado and she gasped, "What are you doing, you fresh thing?"

That seemed a dumb question from any gal who'd come calling on a naked man without any underdrawers on. So he simply parted her soft ample thighs and lowered his hips into her warm love-saddle with his feet braced wide on the rug and growled, "You knew what both of us wanted me to do to you since earlier this evening. So could we just hesh up and let me *do* it before I have to listen to exactly why you changed your mind?"

She laughed out loud, threw her thighs open wider, and grabbed both cheeks of his bare behind to dig her nails in as she thrust up to meet his questing shaft.

As he entered her, deep, he suddenly realized that, whoever this was, it couldn't be Red Robin!

Not that he had any complaints, nor; judging from the way she was bumping and grinding, did she. So a grand time was had by all as they worked together to get her duds off over her head without missing a bump or grind.

It was once they were belly-to-naked-belly in the dark that a man began to suspect there was more to this one than met the eye. Her big old tits felt swell against his bare chest, and there was much to be said for a rump that didn't need even one pillow under it. But this passionately panting total stranger was just plain *fat* anyway you might want to slice her.

He thought a moment and asked uncertainly, "Miss Peony, the upstairs chambermaid?"

To which she replied with a moan and another vaginal contraction, "Who did you think I was, that sissy boy in Room 203? I was just now fixing to leave for the night. I came by to ask if there was anything else I might do for you. I hardly expected to wind up doing *this*, but don't stop now whatever you do!"

So he didn't, and he soon had her moaning, "Oh, Lordy, you're just a dreadful brute and I feel so low and wicked that I just can't thank you enough and I'm cominnng!"

That made two of them, and he sure felt thankful too as they lay there gasping for breath in each other's arms while the fat gal's soft innards kept throbbing with pleasure.

He tended to believe her when she crooned, "My Lord, I haven't been pronged so swell since I left my second husband. He was no damned good either. But I reckon a man who won't work and never wins at cards had to be good at *something*!"

He didn't ask why she'd left her first husband. She'd just told him the second one screwed better. He didn't want to hear another sad tale about getting used and abused by mean menfolk, so he asked if she smoked and when she allowed she did, on the sly, he groped in the dark for that cheroot he'd snuffed out and thumbed a match head to re-light it.

The total stranger smiling awkwardly at him in the flickering glow was younger and prettier than he'd suspected from the width of her bouncy hips and complaints about at least two husbands. Before she could brag on a third, he got their smoke going, shook out the match, and snuggled her closer to ask what she'd meant about Bunny McNee's sissy ways.

She repeated what Matilda had told him in the dining room, then added some lip-smacking noises, now that she knew him well enough to talk dirty. She described young McNee by name, and called the other the strange one, although she made them both sound a tad strange.

She said she'd thought at first they were arguing about money, with McNee bawling like a worried gal that his visitor had said he'd bring some of the next time, which was then. But when she'd moved in closer, to sort of dust the wallpaper closer to McNee's door, the stranger had been saying he wanted his "huggy bunny," which did sound something like *money* when you studied on it. She said McNee had allowed he didn't want to be abused for no good reason by a promise-busting polecat, and that then the stranger had slapped the smaller McNee hard enough to make him cry like a gal some more and promise some mighty vile-sounding tricks that had sounded even sloppier once they'd wound up on the bed.

When Longarm asked how she knew they'd been vile on the bed, Peony giggled and confided, "The bedsprings in Room 203 are the loudest on this floor. I've never gone for that Greek stuff. As I told my first husband, a man too small to enjoy a woman *right* ain't much of a man to begin with. I'll be switched if I can see why any sort of *boy* would be willing to let a man abuse him that way!''

Longarm put the cheroot to her soft lips as he mused, half to himself, ''The younger and smaller riders along the owlhoot trail don't have to be all that willing. Bullies with no respect for the property rights of bankers and railroad stockholders tend to take what they want, when they want it, from anybody they have the edge on. We've been wondering why they had a puny young kid riding along on all those robberies. If they call him Huggy Bunny, that may account for them managing to avoid our usual informants in the whorehouses of many a trail town.''

Peony gave the cheroot back to him as she asked, ''You mean Bunny McNee rides with a band of queer outlaws?''

Longarm blew a thoughtful smokering into the darkness and replied, ''Most lifetime crooks tend to be what the alienists who study queer folks describe as degenerates. Whether they start out favoring gals or not, they spend so much time in prison that they learn how to make love to milk bottles, ham sandwiches, or one another. Old cons like to brag they ain't the ones being queer when they beat up and rape the kid cons they call queers. There's nothing on McNee's yellow sheets, I mean criminal record, about him doing any hard time in state or federal prisons. But I reckon his fellow gang members had learned about such matters during their own misspent youths.''

He took another drag and asked her to describe the one she'd called older and bigger as well as strange.

Peony shrugged a plump shoulder against his bare ribs and said she'd only glimpsed the rascal at a distance, headed the other way down a hallway that was always sort of gloomy. She was sure he'd been dressed cow, in a blue denim jacket and jeans and with a gray hat with its crown pinched higher than most Colorado riders seemed to favor.

Longarm nodded and said, "Some of the gang members are suspected of hailing from Texas. It's a long shot, but they have a dead gun-slick in blue denim on ice in a root cellar down by the jail. Might you be up to viewing the late Ginger Bancott, come morning and less call for the neighbors to gossip about us leaving this hotel together?"

Peony shook her brown curls against his bare shoulder and replied mighty firmly, "I'm not about to be spotted leaving this hotel with you at any hour. I told you I never got a good look at that rascal in the hallway, and didn't somebody say Amos Payne shot that Bancott boy after he'd just shot some Englishman at the depot?"

Longarm nodded. "We might have leaped to a hasty conclusion. We know Ginger Bancott was a professional criminal who'd once killed a man for money down Texas way, and he had on a blue denim outfit as he was gunned right after killing another."

She nodded and said, "Right, that stranger from England."

"Or West-by-God-Virginia!" Longarm cut in. "Stranger is the word to steer by as we move poor Gaylord Stanwyk off the same train I came in on, striding alone into the depot in a suit and tie as well as Stetson and riding boots. After that, we were just about a perfect match as to height and build. I'm not saying we were doubles, but he was the only one who described at all like me, and he was walking alone as I brought up the rear with a bunch of local folks and some baggage!"

Peony marveled, "Good heavens! Are you saying it was *you* that dead boy was out to kill, honey?"

To which he modestly replied, "It wouldn't have been the first time the pals of a crook I was coming for tried to discourage the notion. I can already see a few holes in such a plot. But the jails of this wide country would be less crowded if crooks plotted as smart as me. And besides, who else could have been expecting me? I'd only just wired Constable Payne I was on my way here to transfer a federal prisoner. I didn't know another soul in town, and vice versa.''

She demanded, ''What good would it have done Bunny McNee if a pal *had* murdered the first deputy sent to fetch him? Wouldn't your outfit have simply sent a second, or even a third?''

He sighed and muttered, ''I wish you wouldn't confuse my elaborate plots with simple facts. Are you certain you couldn't help us out in that root cellar, pard? I mean, it's dimly lit, and mayhaps if we sort of rolled him over so's you could view him from behind in dim light . . .''

She sat up, moving the bedsprings considerably, as she swung her button shoes to the rug and said, ''Thanks for reminding me how late I seem to be getting home from work. What time is is, lover?''

Longarm groped his pocket watch from the vest he'd somehow left on the rug on that side and struck another light to declare with a chuckle, ''Lord have mercy if it ain't just going on midnight! I could swear we've known one another at least a full hour, and speaking of knowing one another, in the Biblical sense, how come you're putting on that seersucker uniform so soon? I was fixing to finish this cheroot and suggest a position you may not have ever tried before.''

The pleasantly obese chambermaid sighed wistfully and replied, ''Hold the thought until at least Thursday night. Tomorrow is my day off, and I'd never be able to explain tomorrow night to my husband! For some reason the jealous thing keeps accusing me of fooling with other men when I'm not home picking up after him.''

A big gray cat woke up in Longarm's stomach, swished its bushy tail, sharpened its claws on the roots of his balls, and lay back down, along with his suddenly limp pecker, as he quietly allowed he'd have been much obliged had she told him earlier she was married up.

As she went on pinning her hair with the back of her uniform wide open to her exposed tailbone, Peony giggled and asked if it would have saved her from a ravaging she sure would like to thank him for. Then she asked him to be a lamb and button her up the back. So he lit the bed lamp to do it right, and told her to just hesh when she started to go into her female complaints. For he'd met females who complained they weren't getting enough in the past and he found it tedious to make up self-serving excuses.

What they'd just committed was a sin, and he wasn't going to say her sin was greater than his own because the sinners he kept having to deal with disgusted him with all their talk about only being half-ass siners. A man who stole cows had no call to describe himself as a rustler instead of a cow thief. There was no offense under statute or common law described as rustling, swiping, or helping one's self. What he'd just been doing to another man's wife was described as the state offense of adultery, and it was sure a good thing that wasn't a federal offense. For he was able to just button up her back like a sport without having to consider turning himself in.

But as he did so, he reflected it was sure a good thing he'd be on his way back to Denver with that other sinner come morning. For now he might have at least two jealous jaspers and who knew who else he had to worry about here in John Bull!

Chapter 7

The one and only morning train would be heading down to Golden after nine, lest anyone in town with urgent business miss it. But that still cut too fine for Longarm to find out whether Peony had bragged about him to that waitress pal of hers. Old Matilda would be fixing to start serving in the hotel dining room about the time he had to board that combination with Bunny McNee.

He hadn't wanted to worry about a waitress gal's poker face in any case, and they served tolerable flapjacks with fried eggs at a small joint across from the jail. It was tougher to eat breakfast with your gun hand free and both eyeballs peeled. So he stuffed his own face before he ambled across the way to pick up his prisoner and feed him decently before they headed out. Longarm was too polite to tell local lawmen how to run their own jails. But it was a simple fact that prisoners without pocket jingle to send out for luxuries, such as tobacco and food, got to chew lots of match stems and live on stale bread and unsalted beans in your average small-town lockup.

He found Deputy Rothstein in charge out front. Rothstein allowed his boss, Constable Payne, would be by directly to hand the prisoner over to the federal government on paper. Longarm nodded, but told the amiable younger deputy he wanted to make certain his prisoner got on the train looking well fed and halfway neat.

Rothstein allowed it would be all right to let McNee have some soap and warm water out back while they waited for the constable to get there. Rothstein didn't have any toothbrush for the kid, and razors in the hands of dangerous criminals had never struck him as a sensible suggestion. So Longarm ambled back to the cell block for a word with his prisoner as Rothstein went to tell someone they wanted soap and water from the barbershop next door.

Longarm found Bunny McNee pacing like a caged critter, dressed to go in what looked like a bigger kid's hand-me-downs. The loose jeans and baggy shirt likely were. Longarm told the kid they'd be leaving directly and that it was up to him whether the short day trip down to Denver would be relaxed or tense.

As McNee came to the bars to accept another smoke from the easy-going Longarm, he nervously asked just what that meant.

Longarm flared a match to light them both up as he tersely said, "You can ride down to Denver like a passenger who just happens to be headed for a hearing before a federal judge, or you can ride all the way in handcuffs and leg irons. I can be as fair or as firm as the situation calls for and . . . Hold on now, Bunny. Don't we have you on yellow foolscap as a wayward youth of nineteen, going on twenty?"

The youthful prisoner shrugged and replied, "What if you do?"

To which Longarm soberly replied, as Rothstein came to join them with a remark about that soap and water, "You don't need a shave."

Rothstein had naturally heard that. So he said, "I told you why we don't allow no razors back here unsupervised. Our swamper will be here with that soap and water as soon as it heats up next door. You say the punk don't need any shave to begin with?"

Longarm gravely nodded and told the prisoner, "I'd like you to unbutton that floppy shirt and show us your hairy chest now. I'd as soon you kept your pants on, though."

Bunny McNee primly replied, "I don't want to unbutton my shirt for you. I was raised to be more modest than most, and since when is it a crime for a boy to have a bare chest?"

Longarm smiled thinly and said, "I've yet to see a boy with any sort of chest go all this jail time without even sprouting some lip fuzz, if he's really a boy of nineteen. So about them buttons . . ."

McNee stamped a boot heel on the cement and sort of sobbed, "All right, if you must know, I'm not a boy. I'm a girl. I've been a sort of tomboy girl for all of those nine-teen years you mentioned. Are you satisfied?"

Longarm sighed and said, "A lawman transferring a prisoner just ain't allowed to get satisfied with her. I owe my poor old boss an apology. I thought he'd assigned two deputies to transport you down to Denver because he didn't want one of 'em to go to a dance. Now I suspect he knew, or suspected, more than I did about you when I changed Marshal Vail's orders behind his back!"

Turning to Rothstein, Longarm continued. "Let her have the soap and water, but don't plan on her *going* anywhere today. I have to send me another telegram. There's no way in hell I can get me another deputy and a matron from the federal house of detention up this way before I'm stuck for at least one more night up here. For I ain't about to spend the better part of a day alone with a prisoner of the female

63

persuasion and an established lying nature!''

The poor excuse for a youth on the far side of the bars blew a teasing puff of smoke and coyly asked, ''Why, Deputy Long, are you saying you can't be trusted not to abuse my fair white body?''

Longarm snorted, ''I'm saying you can't be trusted not to accuse me the moment we get you before a federal grand jury. But since you had to ask, I wouldn't abuse you with Ginger Bancott's dick, you skinny lying two-bit slut!''

She asked who Bancott was as Longarm stormed out, composing one mighty humble telegram in his worried mind. There was no damned way he could wire his home office without eating a generous helping of crow. But it likely served him right for being such a smart-ass in the first place. Some antique Greek had written, years before, how those frisky Greek gods in fig leaves and firemen's helmets liked to totally screw mere mortals up by making them feel smarter than they could ever really be!

A man strode fast in low-heeled boots when he was as chagrined as a Turkish pasha with a big harem and a little dick. So he'd sent his sheepish wire and was coming back out of the Western Union near the depot when Constable Payne caught up with him.

Payne said, ''Nate Rothstein told me. It wasn't easy, but we got the prisoner's pants down and she sure is a hairy little thing down in the cornfield where the sun but seldom shines! Are you saying none of you federal lawmen *knew* why that outlaw gang had her tagging along to hold their horses and doubtless other things for 'em?''

Longarm grimaced and replied, ''She fooled *you* gents, didn't she? Let's cut across to yonder saloon and wet our whistles as we gossip about the lady in some shade.''

Constable Payne thought that made more sense than anything else he'd heard since coming to work that morning.

As they bellied up to the bar inside, Payne signaled for two needled beers and confided, "Nate Rothstein thinks she might be a ringer. I used to play chess when the game was checkers too. The kid reads too many of them dime detective magazines."

Longarm waited until the barkeep slid their schooners across the zinc-topped bar to them before he observed, "Who's to say Nate might not have a point?"

Payne said, "Me. I was the arresting officer, in broad daylight, when the narrow-gauge backed up from that landslide to deliver an apparent deadbeat into the hands of the law. The charges had been pressed by Manager Cooper at the Elk Rack Hotel you just checked out of. We didn't know, then, we had more than a simple vagrancy and theft-of-service charge on him—I mean her. So what would all sorts of razzle-dazzle be meant to accomplish, if Nate's notion is supposed to make a lick of sense?"

Longarm sipped some beer needled with fair rye as he considered, and then asked, "That hotel manager pressed charges against the one you've been holding, of course?"

Payne snorted, "The sass never owed *me* nothing! Naturally Cooper bore witness before Silas Hall, our justice of the peace. We don't lock drifters up just for the hell of it. We had her locked up as a he who'd skipped out on a hotel bill until it was Nate, I'll have to allow, who noticed we had a possible federal want on our hands."

Payne sipped at his own schooner, set it down again, and said with a weary smile, "I told you Nate reads a lot. I thought from the tone of Marshal Vail's telegram that he'd be sending a deputy who knew the notorious Bunny McNee on sight."

Longarm considered, shook his head, and replied, "I doubt either of the original team knew Bunny any better than me, and I never laid eyes on him, her or it until I got here yesterday.''

Payne said, ''Nate tells me you tried to trick the sneaky gal with a remark about the late Ginger Bancott. He says that after you left she asked about that, and acted surprised but not at all upset when Nate told her the tale about the shootout at the depot. Nate says that if she'd ever known Ginger Bancott, she was one hell of an actress.''

Longarm snorted and replied, ''We've established that she's one hell of an actress. How many gals have you ever met who could stay at a hotel as a man and convince a snoopy chambermaid she was at worst a sissy? After that, we have dozens of witnesses who identified the kid holding the getaway mounts for the gang as a wayward youth of the male persuasion.''

Payne sipped some suds thoughtfully, then said, ''Six of one and half a dozen of the other. Say she come up here to hide out with Ginger or somebody else when the gang split up after their last big haul. There's only the one hotel, but a *real* wayward youth could hole up any number of places as a hired hand or paying boarder. So say Ginger or whoever cached his sweeter sidekick in the Elk Rack lest somone notice she sat down to pee, or simply to keep anyone from noticing *two* strangers in town all at once.''

Longarm grimaced and said, ''I thought you just advised against a chess game we don't really have to play. I told you I'd sent for chaperones. Once I have her before Judge Dickerson with no counter-charges to offer, he's fixing to tell her she can tell all she knows or face a slow twenty years in striped cotton dress. Females have fewer good years to spend than us, and twenty years would scare a heap of men. But since she never actually aimed a gun at anyone as a member of that meaner bunch, Judge Dickerson could doubtless let her walk, if she was willing to witness against rascals who let her down and left her stranded with an unpaid hotel bill.''

Payne nodded soberly and said, ''I follow your drift. But what if Ginger Bancott wasn't that other robber she was hiding out with? My boys have been scouting about to no avail trying to find out where *he* was holed up before he tried for either you or that Englishman at the depot across the way.''

Longarm shrugged and replied, ''I've been studying on that angle. At the risk of false modesty, the more I study the more I tend to go with Gaylord Stanwyk as the intended target. I ain't the only gent who ever trod on somebody else's toes, and way more folk knew *he* was on his way to John Bull. You and your deputies were the only ones in town I wired that I'd be coming in place of them other deputies.''

Amos Payne stared goggle-eyed and gasped, ''Thunderation! Are you suggesting me or mine could have been out to gun the transferring lawman before he could take our pretty prisoner away from us?''

Longarm said, ''The thought had occurred to me. But . . .''

''Then that's the dumbest thought I ever heard tell of, and you'd be surprised what I hear from the drunks on payday night! Had we been aiming to aid and abet the escape of Bunny McNee, we'd have just let her go and say she escaped! That don't sound half as risky for a bought-off town constable as assassinating federal agents! I suppose you're fixing to tell me next that I hired that known killer to kill you and then killed him when he killed the wrong man?''

Longarm snorted and growled, ''I hadn't finished. I was saying I like to ponder all the possibles before I make up my mind. So I did and, had you let me finish, I was about to make them very points for you all.''

''We never had to wire you people we were holding a federal want to begin with!'' Payne whined. ''We'd only arrested a deadbeat drifter as far as anyone else in town knew. Had the shiftless slut been rich enough to bribe this child, she'd have paid way less to the Elk Rack Hotel and never been arrested in the first place!''

Longarm nodded, drained the last of his schooner, and replied in a friendlier way, ''That does make that tall Englishman the far more likely target. Might you have a public library here in John Bull, old son?''

Payne looked surprised, then said, ''Sort of. That limey mining syndicate built a school with a library wing whilst this was their company town. Now that we've incorporated as a Colorado township, the school, library, and such are still there, no matter who's been paying for their upkeep. You sure bring up a heap of matters nobody's ever asked me about before.''

Longarm said, ''They pay me to be nosy. Which way did you say your schoolhouse was?''

Payne said to head away from the mining operation and railroad yards until he passed the First Methodist Church. The frame school complex would be back from the road a piece, surrounded by shade trees of green ash. So they shook on it and parted friendly. It wasn't easy, but Amos Payne managed not to ask what Longarm wanted with a library.

But others were more suspicious of Longarm's motives as they watched from the shade of a shop overhang at a respectful distance.

The man who'd met with the Widow Farnsworth's maid asked the more respectable-looking man next to him, ''Where do you reckon that nosy lawman could be headed now? That morning train will be leaving for Golden any

68

minute now, and he ain't got that prisoner out of jail yet!''

The man in position to give the orders said, ''Follow him. Let's hope for his sake it's some last-minute errand. You're right about that train. That's not all we'll be right about if he fails to catch it out of here. They warned us he was a sly fox who plays with his cards close to his vest!''

The more obvious gunslick grinned wolfishly and said, ''I told you I thought he was fibbing to that widow gal in her very own parlor! Do I get to gun him if he fails to get aboard that train?''

To which his boss replied in a disgusted tone, ''Why, no, I wanted you to get him hot with some Frenching whilst the rest of us drop our pants, bend over, and spread our cheeks! If he was never really sent up our way to carry that saddle tramp back to Denver, he was sent to pester somebody else, and we're the only action for miles that any federal lawman could be interested in, Quicksilver!''

The one known as Quicksilver Quinn to those who rented his gun hand at the going rate purred, ''I've never had the chance to gun anyone really famous before. I don't want to see my real name there. But I'm fixing to save the newspaper clippings to show my grandchildren some fine day. How do you reckon they got on to us, though?''

The older man shrugged and said, ''If they were really on to us they'd be up here in force, making some arrests. They can't have all that much on anybody yet.''

He took a deep breath, sighed, and said, ''I hear that train a'coming from the roundhouse now. That son of a bitch is still on his nosy way to somewheres else. You know what to do. I'd hold my fire till that Shay locomotive goes chugging and clanking past.''

To which Quicksilver Quinn could only modestly reply, ''Don't tell your granny how to suck eggs, or this child how to kill a man!''

Chapter 8

The small town wasn't old enough for planted trees to grow as big as the handsome grove of green ash off to the east of the cinder-paved man street. So Longarm knew somebody sensible had chosen a handsome site to build on, a tad off center, to leave as many old shade trees as possible for the mighty sunny mountain summers. The green ash dropped its leaves in the fall just as some cooler sunshine would feel right for the kids in the yard during recess play.

The little rascals were enjoying their summer vacations as he strode up to the doorway of the barn-red main building. But as he'd hoped, there were grownups working there all summer.

A little gal in a print dress with a pencil stuck in the bun of her upswept mouse-brown hair looked scared of the federal badge he showed her, until he told her he hadn't come to arrest anyone for not cleaning the blackboards right. She led him along a corridor as she told him their school library was only for the use of the pupils and their teachers, but that he could borrow all the books he wanted without any lending library card.

He assured her he only wanted to paw through their latest

copies of the Encyclopedia Britannica if they had a set on hand.

The mouse said, "Of course we have. I just told you it was a school library. What was it you wanted to look up?"

Knowing she was most likely trying to be helpful, there being about two dozen volumes in the set arranged alphabetically, he politely replied, "Railroads, or railways as the British call 'em. Either way, they ought to be listed under R. But I reckon I ought to take a gander at Civil Engineering under C as long as I'm here. This sure is a handsome school you got here, ma'am. The tax rolls of your average town this size can't afford anything this grand. It was put up by that original mining syndicate, right?"

The mousy little teacher, principal, or whatever sniffed and said, "It was. Now it's maintained for the most part by Widow Farnsworth, who runs the railroad and isn't half as stingy with her money as the new board of aldermen and that cowboy who thinks he's a mayor. What you said about them taxing freeholders for education was, alas, all too true! Lord knows what we'd do, or who'd ever educate children, if it wasn't for Widow Farnsworth!"

As she led him into a spacious reading room with a bigger chamber filled with book stacks off to one side, Longarm sniffed at the pine oil some tidy soul had been cleaning with and said, "I met up with Widow Farnsworth just last evening, ma'am. I could see right off she was a handsome woman. I didn't know she was *this* handsome, even though I'm here this morning on her behalf."

The schoolmarm naturally asked, as she led the way back to rustle up the two tomes he meant to start with, what Widow Farnsworth could have to do with the Encyclopedia Britannica. So he told her about that English railroading man's untimely death.

As they found the volumes he needed he explained:

"Stanwyk told Widow Farnsworth he might have a simple solution for some problems she can't find any American railroaders to fix. I have the advantage of being an American with an open mind on railroading. I know the way we lay track seems a heap more sensible. I want to see if a hunch I had last night about the more complicated English way makes sense to the wise old birds they hire to write all this stuff."

They put the two volumes on a shellacked oak reading table and, as he got out his notebook and a pencil stub, she protested, "Heavens, we can do better than that. Wait right here and I'll fetch you some colored pencils and graph paper. You do mean to copy down some railroading diagrams, don't you?"

He said he sure did. So she left him there alone as, outside, the morning train he'd meant to leave aboard with Bunny McNee went puffing and banging by.

He set his Stetson aside on the table and broke open the logical first choice. He found page after page of railroad lore. He flipped pages to determine how long he was apt to be stuck here, and then it hit him, smack between the eyes at first glance. So he said, "Hot dice on payday! That has to be it!" as he grinned down at a side-by-side comparison of American Stevens and British Wilkinson rails in cross section. The clear line cuts, showing how each brand was held securely down to the cross ties, were easy enough to memorize without making one's own sketches.

But out in the hallway, the mousy Miss Dorman of the John Bull Grammar School had been headed back to the reading room with the drawing materials she'd promised when she was grabbed roughly from behind and let out a mousy squeak before Quicksilver Quinn had his gun muzzle in one ear and was growling into the other, "Hesh your face and do as I say! I don't aim to rob you and you ain't worth the time and trouble of a rape. I only need some guidance. That lawman you was talking to out front was not where I thought he'd be as that train went by just now. So where's he at and what's he doing?''

She gulped and gasped, ''You're hurting me! Deputy Long's not doing anything to anybody in our reading room. He just came to look something up. He couldn't be after *you*. So why don't you just run away while you have the chance?''

The gunslick ground the muzzle of his gun against the tender flesh of her ear and demanded, ''Show me the way as I sort of ride you piggyback with this other arm around your waist. How come you're wearing a corset, girl? You're as lightly built as one of your schoolgals!''

Miss Dorman had never considered herself a brave young woman. But she tried to dig her heels in, and when that didn't work, she tried to steer them the wrong way at the first fork in the corridor. But the experienced gunslick growled, ''I reckon we'll just head *thissaways*! Is yonder archway the way into this here reading room?''

It was, but Miss Dorman didn't answer. Quicksilver chuckled and murmured, ''You're fixing to help me whether you aim to or not. You ain't big enough to stop many bullets. But all I need is the moment of hesitation you'll inspire when he sees you betwixt us. Get moving and don't struggle no more. I mean it!''

So in point of fact the burly killer was half carrying the weaker schoolmarm as they came in together fast, with the killer's six-gun out of her ear and trained dead ahead.

Seeing nothing but Longarm's Stetson on the heavy oaken table, Quicksilver fired and sent the hat flying before he'd grasped that nobody seemed to be wearing it.

He still figured his target had dropped down out of sight behind that natural cover. So that was the direction he was

73

staring when Longarm made his own move.

Having just replaced the two heavy volumes where they belonged, Longarm had been returning to the reading room from among the stacks when he'd heard the muffled sounds of the struggle out yonder and drawn his own double-action .44-40. So he had a sideways shot at a burly target advancing behind a skinny shield, and not wanting to risk the mousy little gal, he aimed high and fired without warning.

Two hundred grains of hot spinning lead went in one of Quicksilver's temples and burst out the other with a teacup's worth of blood and brains as the schoolmarm broke loose to wind up facedown on that reading table screaming fit to bust!

Longarm lowered his smoking muzzle, but held on to the grips in case these critters hunted in pairs. He could see at a glance the hunting days were over for the rascal he'd spread across the floor like a bear rug. So he moved to comfort the terrified gal.

"It's over, ma'am." he said, placing a gentle free hand on one sobbing shoulder. "They'd have heard that gunshot back up the street. So other lawmen will soon be here whether you keep bawling for them or not, hear?"

She gasped, "He was going to murder you! He told me so! He said I wasn't pretty enough for a fate worse than death, but I just knew he was going to kill me too!"

Longarm shot another glance at the dead man at their feet, grimaced in distaste, and allowed, "You were likely right about that last part, and I wouldn't have bet on the first. You're a right nice-looking gal and he'd have never brought the topic up if it hadn't crossed his mind."

She stopped crying and demurely said, "Why, thank you. That was an awfully nice thing to say."

Chapter 9

It was possible to gun a man and get out of town without further formality, but outside of a Ned Buntline romance of a Wilder West, it wasn't considered proper. So Longarm explained how pressed for time he'd be once some chaperons arrived from Denver, and the dentist who sat in for the county coroner up at that end of the county set the hearing for that very afternoon.

The coroner's sub-panel met in the town hall facing the dusty municipal corral. Twelve men good and true lined up along one side of a trestle table to call the shots. Most everyone else of any importance around John Bull got to watch from the folding seats set up for their enjoyment. The layout sort of reminded Longarm of a play or graduation ceremony, but their star, the late Quicksilver Quinn, had graduated to his own bed of ice in that root cellar with what was likely a dead associate called Ginger Bancott.

The identity of the villain Longarm had gunned had been established on the scene by Deputy Rothstein, who seemed to read nothing but old wanted fliers. Miss Dorman from the schoolhouse appeared before the sub-panel as their first witness, ladies first, to primly establish the dead man had been using her as a shield and whispering villainous threats to her as he'd fired the first shot and been shot at in turn. The mousy little gal didn't have to say anything about fates worse than death. Quicksilver Quinn had been wanted on that charge as well.

Constable Payne and Deputy Rothstein were only asked a few questions as to what they'd found when they tore down the street towards those distant but distinct gunshots. Neither charged Longarm with raping Miss Dorman or gunning anybody but Quinn, of course. So their terse statements were taken down too, and then it was Longarm's turn.

For some reason there came a round of applause from the onlookers as he rose to take his place before the sub-panel. As he sat himself on the bentwood witness chair he spied many a familiar face in the crowd and nobody looked sore at him. He saw all those folks he'd come up on the narrow-gauge with, save for the small kids who'd been with Flora Munro, present and accounted for.

Widow Farnsworth was there, and to Longarm's chagrin, so was fat Peony from his hotel, with a skinny galoot that had to be her jealous husband. But at least Longarm didn't see that asshole kid who'd warned him to stay away from young Flora Munro.

The dentist in charge of the hearings swore him in, heard him out as he gave his own laconic account of the reading room shootout, and then demanded to know why Quinn had been gunning for him.

Longarm answered simply, "I don't know. Didn't know who he was before Nate Rothstein nudged my memory by describing the remains on the schoolhouse floor more formally. I was just minding my own beeswax with the En-cyclopedia Britannica when, like Miss Dorman says, Quinn busted in with her to shoot my hat. So I naturally shot him."

There was a murmur of approval along the table as well as from the crowd behind him. Then a crusty older gent in a snuff-colored frock coat demanded to know what Longarm had been looking for in those "sissy furrin books."

Longarm started to tell them. Then he reflected that the pretty Constance Farnsworth would have to call to serve him more tea and pastry if he solved her problem here and now, like a jackass with better things to do and fancier places to go that evening. They'd have never asked what he'd been up to if he'd said he was killing a morning in a card house or saloon, damn 'em. So he shrugged and said, "I like to read schoolbooks when I have time on my hands. My formal education was cut short by the war. But there's all sorts of book learning there, just for the reading."

Another old-timer, dressed more country, snorted, "That'll be the day when this child wastes the little time the Good Lord gives us on book learning! I say ride out across the hills and see it all for your ownselves! See sky-scraping mountains white with summer snow and wide valley carpeted with blue-eyed grass for as far as you can see!"

The dentist said, "Simmer down, Oregon John. This is an inquest, not a poetry reading, and you heard the man say he likes to read for the pleasure of it."

Then he asked Longarm if it seemed possible the killer had been out to prevent a federal lawman from carrying out his more important chores.

Longarm truthfully replied, "As Constable Payne just told you, I was sent up here to pick up a federal want he'd arrested on a petty local charge."

An onlooker near the front of the crowd called out, "The hell you say! That McNee boy owed us better than a month's wages for an honest cowhand in unpaid room and board!''

Longarm assumed the florid-faced older man had to be the manager of the Elk Rack. Half turning in his chair, he nodded and called out, "I meant petty next to the federal charges hanging over him and his pals, Mister Cooper. After that, he wasn't any boy. He, or I ought to say *she,* appears to have ridden with them other outlaws as a doxie, as such wicked ladies are described along the owlhoot trail.''

Turning back to the sub-panel as the crowd buzzed like a beehive, Longarm continued. "We had just determined the gender of the prisoner an hour or so before Quinn came gunning for me. I have no call, in a chamber half filled with ladies, to go into why I thought it unwise to head back to Denver unchaperoned with a wicked lady. Suffice it to say I wired my home office for some safety in numbers, and then I was stuck for at least another day up your way, no offense. So with so much time on my hands I ambled on down to the school, where Miss Dorman, yonder, was kind enough to let me kill some of said time, and the next thing I knew I was killing Quicksilver Quinn. I understand he liked to be called Quicksilver because he was so fast as well as unpedictable. If any of you have ever spilt real quicksilver from a thermometer, you've seen how it darts all about like spit on a hot stove as soon as you try to sweep it up.''

The dentist in charge sighed and asked what basic chemistry had to do with a killer's possible motivation.

Longarm said, "Nothing, save for the fact he prided himself on being hard to figure. You'd have to ask the jokers who sent him after me what their motive might have been. Quicksilver is in no position to say, and he never said a word to me on his way to the floor.''

That little old lady who'd come up on the narrow-gauge with him rose to shake a bony fist and shout, "Cow thieves! That's what they have to be! I've lost four head in the last month and both them dead boys in that root cellar died with cowboy boots on their shiftless feet!"

The dentist said, "Sit down, Granny Boggs. Lots of riders wear cowboy boots. It don't signify nothing."

The peppery old lady snapped, "It signifies they knew how to herd cows, and I can tell you for a fact neither one was working anywhere in these parts as a cowhand. I asked!"

The dentist rolled his eyes skyward and marveled, "All I want to record is the facts that are known and I get blue-eyed grass, the Encyclopedia Britannica, and strayed or stolen beef! It's a fact both those dead strangers had no known address, visible means of support, or honest reasons to be up our way to begin with. After that, they both had criminal records."

"As hired guns!" Granny Boggs chimed in. "So who hired 'em if it wasn't some untidy neighbors stealing stock off the rest of us?"

There came a low rumble of suspicion, if not agreement. The man in the snuff-colored outfit called out, "Let's rein in and eat this apple at a bite at a time! A lot of folks have lost stock to the vicious wet thaw this spring, and I'm not saying no trash nesters couldn't have helped themselves to some prime veal since. But we've long since been agreed nobody could move enough beef out to matter without loading it aboard the narrow-gauge, which they ain't."

The dentist called out, "Would you care to chime in, Widow Farnsworth?"

But the Junoesque Constance Farnsworth only called back a demure agreement to the agreement just cited. She said her railroad had only carried a modest amount of beef and a lot more produce and stamped ore to market. When she added everything loaded aboard her combination was recorded as to shipper and receiver down in Golden, the dentist cum deputy coroner banged for attention and ruled that, as in the case of the late Ginger Bancott, the late Quicksilver Quinn had been properly gunned in the line of duty by a paid-up lawman and that, after that, what either desperado had been up to, six-gun blazing, would be left an open question until some damned body came forward with some more sensible answers than any suggested so far.

That stuck Longarm as a sensible finding, and he said so as he got up from his chair, dismissed as a witness. He was now more convinced that both gun waddies had been after him in particular, meaning poor Gaylord Stanwyk had been mistaken for him at the depot the day before. But seeing he'd already looked into what Stanwyk had come up there to look into, he elbowed his way through the milling crowd to catch up with the brunette railroading gal on the town hall steps.

When he told her he'd been studying on railroad track, she told him he'd be having supper with her that evening, if he could manage to get there by seven. Fashionable folks ate later than working folks. He'd read that the beautiful but scatter-headed Princess Alexandra of Wales ate her supper at *eight*! That likely accounted for the slimmer figures of older society matrons. The poor things tore through life sidesaddle, half starved.

In the time he had left that afternoon, Longarm sent more wires of inquiry about both boys in that root cellar, and made sure his federal prisoner would be served a warm supper from that beanery across from the jail. They took his money before they told him Constable Payne had already been ordering three meals a day for that young outlaw he'd arrested. But Longarm took this like a sport. He was only out four bits, and it was good to hear old Amos Payne was a sport as well. Longarm had always had a low opinion of lawmen who cheated the taxpaying public at the expense of the crooks they were paid to feed.

He'd never planned on more than twenty-four hours in John Bull when he'd left Denver traveling so light. He'd been fibbing when he threatened Bunny McNee with leg irons. He had one set of handcuffs hooked to the back of his gun rig, but after that, he hadn't even brought along his shaving kit. So he found a barber still open as the shadows lengthened, and sat down to wait his turn. He figured he could manage a good bath at the hotel, and he hadn't sweated up his shirt, socks, or underpants too bad in this cool dry mountain air, but there was no getting around a stubble too noteworthy to take to a sit-down supper with a high-toned widow woman.

Barbershops tended to be small-town gossip shops as well. As a rule it was best to just listen. But when he spied the old-timer they called Oregon John just one stool down, he naturally commenced a conversation with the man, who doubtless knew these hills far better than he did. As the barber worked on the customer ahead of them, Longarm got Oregon John off the two dead owlhoot riders to riders in general around John Bull. In a desperately casual tone, Longarm said, "I know they say that old lady, Granny Boggs, is a mite overwrought on the subject of cow thieves, but I know for a fact that an old pal of mine lit out for higher country aboard a mule this very morning. Mention was made of a cross-country trail to the newer gold fields around Holy Cross on the far side of the Divide."

Oregon John stared dreamily and intoned, "I've seen that mystical mountain with a holy cross of summer snow outlined against its dark brooding granite. They say the Rocky

Mountain cross-beak bird got its poor bitty beak bent up that way from trying in vain to pull the nails from that big holy cross to free Our Lord from his suffering!''

The barber shot Longarm a knowing look. Longarm said he was sorry as hell about cross-beak birds, but that he'd asked about trails out of these parts with a view to driving stolen cows along them.

Oregon John replied less poetically, "A good drover can drive a cow most anywhere he can ride a horse, I reckon. But where in thunder would he want to drive 'em up here in the high country?''

Longarm answered flatly, "The mining camp of Holy Cross, a tad south of that interesting mountain. I was over yonder just a spell back, and I know for a fact they've been paying top wages and eating prime beef. Some other pals of mine made a handsome profit out of driving a modest herd to Holy Cross. I rid with 'em and helped just a mite during surly weather. *Those* cows had all been lawful bought and paid for on this side of the Divide, of course.''

Oregon John said, "Nobody but Granny Boggs says any cows have left this park *any* way. She's right about every stock outfit losing heavy to this spring's thaw. I could show you one hell of a mess of scattered beef bones if you'd care to ride the slopes all about with me. But ain't nobody been herding cows out of here the hard way. I ain't saying a dishonest cowboy *couldn't,* seeing how it might look to ship beef by rail wearing someone else's brand. But I have been over those surrounding slopes more than most—searching for color more than cow turds, it's true—and I regret to say Granny Boggs is an old crazy lady. I'd buy her seeing real men under her bed than this gang of cow thieves she keeps telling the rest of us to watch out for!''

The barber volunteered, "Oregon's right about the severe spring die-off. I have heaps of customers in the beef industry. They tell me they risk the awful weather up our way because, when it ain't killing cows, it feeds 'em much fatter than the warmer but drier High Plains to the east.''

Longarm nodded and said, ''Beef critters growing up on greener grass and juicy sedges sell for way more a head and tend to be sold closer to home to local butchers. Meaning we're talking about fewer head to the smaller mountain herds, and fewer to steal at a higher profit if that temptation should lead you astray. But you gents surely know more than me about your local beef industry.''

The barber said, ''Next!'' as he spun the man he'd been shaving around to let him up. As the customer rose, Longarm saw it was that gent from the hearing in that snuff-colored suit. As their eyes met the older man nodded and said, ''I thought we'd agreed those killers were after *you*, Deputy Long.''

Longarm shrugged and said, ''Like the old hymn says, 'Farther along we'll know more about it.' I'd still like to know where either of those old boys had been hiding out before poor Stanwyk and me seem to have flushed 'em.''

The snuff suit put his hat back on and grumped out with a remark about being late for supper. Longarm expected Oregon John to go next, but the barber explained the old-timer just liked to sit and gossip there. So Longarm took a seat in the still-warm barber's chair and casually asked who that older jasper might have been.

The barber allowed he'd been Mister T.S. Nabors of Colorado Consolidated Holdings. He didn't know what the T.S. stood for.

Oregon John said, ''I can tell you. It stands for Tough Shit. He's the big hoorah of that holding company that bought out the original English mining outfit. They were all right, but C.C.H. wants to own everything profitable and let anything else wither on the vine.''

As the barber cranked Longarm back and draped him with seersucker he grumbled, "When you're right you're right, Oregon John. Them silver-mining Englishmen built everything from that railroad to a handsome company town for their mostly Cornish mining men. But now it's all headed for hell in a hack. You want a haircut too, Deputy Long?"

Longarm said just a shave. So the barber covered his face with a hot wet towel, complaining, "First they cut wages as the ore body started to go low-grade on 'em. So naturally a heap of the better and higher-paid miners quit. I mean, I've never drilled hardrock for *any* sort of ore, but it can't be fair to ask a man to mine more rock for less money, no matter what the infernal rock is worth!"

Longarm was in no position to comment, but Oregon John, bless him, said, "That's the way they pay mining men. It surely causes a heap of labor agitation. I talked to some of the Cousin Jacks as they were fixing to move on. Longarm there is right about them paying better over in Holy Cross, or even down Leadville way. It's gotten worse, since that outfit old T.S. runs moved in on us. They've cut wages in the ore-stamping plant as well, even though you have to stamp a heap more lead ore than silver ore to show the same profit."

Longarm was bursting to ask. But he didn't have to when old Oregon John said he'd heard C.C.H. was trying to buy out Widow Farnsworth, doubtless to cut railroad wages and raise fares and freight rates.

The barber said, "I doubt she wants to sell out, though."

To which Oregon John soberly replied, "Don't matter what the lady might want. The Carsons didn't want to sell them water rights they'd dammed on their own land neither. But just the same, they *sold* 'em, at T.S. Nabors' price!"

Chapter 10

Longarm was glad he'd sprung for that shave and asked for extra bay rum as soon as he got back up to the Farnsworth house. For his Junoesque brunette hostess had on a blue satin gown fit to join the President for supper at the White House. They each got to sit at opposite ends of a long table, with the room lit up by bright, expensive, whale-wax candles, and were served by an old confounded-looking gal with a Cornish lilt to her timid voice as she asked whether she'd served enough candied sweet taters with his lamb.

Constance Farnsworth was nice to her, but as soon as she'd left the dining room Constance confided, ''She's new. At any formal serving, I mean. I was forced to hire her on short notice this very afternoon. But I fear she needed the job even more than I needed a new maid. So I'm sure it will work out.''

Longarm said, ''She served me decent enough, ma'am. I noticed that younger gal who was here last night wasn't dishing out the grub this evening.''

His hostess frowned thoughtfully and replied, ''I can't understand it. Sarah said nothing about giving notice. She was upstairs, dusting, when our morning train left for the outside world. So she has to be somewhere nearby. But none of my other help has been able to locate the silly thing and, in all modesty, I do have some help on my payroll.''

Longarm said, "She's likely hiding out on you, then. Have you looked to see if you'd be missing any valuables, ma'am? Help quitting without notice have been known to leave with milady's jewels, the family silver, or the best pony out back, whether they were sore at their boss or not.''

The comely widow sighed and said, "There's nothing of value missing. You're not the only reluctant cynic at this table. But it does seem she packed her best things and slipped out the back way just after noon. She was serving a noonday guest and me when we got word of your gunfight down at the school. I was naturally concerned for the safety of poor Beth Dorman too. But from the way Sarah carried on and burst right into the conversation, I gathered she knew our school principal even better than I do. I told Sarah I'd tell her all the details as soon as I got back from that hearing at the town hall, but by the time I'd returned, she'd packed up and slipped out like a thief in broad daylight. I've no idea why.''

Longarm said, "That makes two of us. This mint jelly sure goes swell with this lamb, ma'am. As soon as we're done here, I got the answer to another mystery we were talking about. I looked up English railroad trackage at that school this morning, in hopes of figuring out what Gaylord Stanwyk had in mind for your narrow-gauge. I got some pencil sketches I made at my hotel, just before I headed up this way. I'd be proud to show 'em to you, after you've had your dessert.''

Constance Farnsworth rang a small brass bell by her own plate, and when that miner's woman came in she allowed they'd have their dessert and more tea served in her parlor.

Then she rose to her feet and asked Longarm what was keeping him.

He followed her sheepishly into her parlor, hauling out the drawings he'd made on hotel stationery as she quickly led the way. Seeing she seemed so anxious, he sat right down beside her and forked over the drawings, saying, "You told both that civil engineer and me why you couldn't afford to lay all those miles of new track for a marginally profitable mountain line. I suspect Stanwyk found it as odd that a cheap holding company, salvaging a played-out boom at bargain prices, wanted to pay *anything* for a railroad that needed a total overhaul."

She stared down at the diagrams he'd drawn from memory, shaking her puzzled head as she said, "They have some of that English rail on hand. Not nearly enough to replace my whole line, even if they were willing to sell it to me."

She held Longarm's sketches up to better light, adding, "What am I missing here? Everyone knows English and American rails are different. That's why I can't use the cheaper American rails to rebuild my worn and battered English rails, Deputy Long."

He said, "My friends call me Custis. Those dumbbell-shaped or double Wilkinson rails running the whole length of your line have to rest in those little grippers because they'd never stand up to the weight of a train if they were just gripped by spike heads American style."

She said she could see that, and that her late husband had once allowed it seemed a complicated way to lay railroad tracks.

He said, "I suspect few Englishmen have bothered to study on it. Folks tend to accept what they're used to without studying on why it ought to *be* that way. I must be nosier than most. When something makes no sense to me

I like to see if I can find out why."

He leaned closer to point at the way the English rail was bedded down as he explained. "Those fancy fasteners that hold Wilkinson rails to what Englishmen call *sleepers* instead of cross ties are way more expensive than the four spikes and at most a flat plate that we use. The Englishmen who lay tracks ain't dumb. They figure their fancier fittings pay for themselves with change to spare when the top riding surface gets worn and they simply loosen the bolts and *turn the rail over,* with the worn side down and the identical-shaped fresh side up!"

For a gal who'd only inherited a railroad from a man who'd never built one, Constance Farnsworth caught on quickly. She gasped, "My God, no wonder they killed poor Gaylord! He was about to save me a king's ransom! All my track workers have to do, for a few furlongs every day, is loosen those bolts, pull a section of rail up, and simply drop it back in place upside down!"

"They have to tighten the bolts before you run any trains across your new riding surfaces, though," he quietly warned.

She was beaming at him radiantly as she gushed, "It's so simple, yet so logical, even if it sounds too good to be true! But if only poor Gaylord had simply told me all this down in Denver, he might have still been alive!"

Longarm nodded soberly and replied, "He might have hoped for some greater reward if he made it seem he'd put more effort into it. You hear sad tales from folks who feel somebody took a grand notion from them and never considered sharing the wealth when it paid off. I met this old coot who used to work back East in Tom Edison's invention factory."

He leaned back. "I doubt the old coot invented that electric lamp like he said he did. But my point is that a man with a sudden bright but simple notion might be worried about getting paid for it.''

The older Cornish woman came in with the dessert and tea service. When she'd managed not to spill any of it, the widow said *she'd* serve and the old gal backed out awkwardly.

As soon as they were alone again, the pretty young widow quietly asked what Longarm thought she might owe him for saving her derriere—a fancy word for ass.

Longarm laughed lightly and said he was a deputy marshal, not a civil engineer. He added, ''Like I told them at that hearing this afternoon, I had time on my hands and nothing better to do. The only reason I never said what I'd been looking up was that you might have had some business rivals there. I found out at the barbershop I was on the money about that. Old T.S. Nabors of C.C.H. was sitting on that panel like he already owned this whole park.''

She sliced him some marble cake as she softly said, ''I'm still in deep debt to you, ah, Custis. I don't know what poor Gaylord Stanwyk meant to demand of me for the same simple but important help. I don't know what I can do for you, if you won't accept even a token percentage of the money you'll be saving me.''

He said an extra helping of her swell cake would do him fine.

She blinked at his empty saucer and murmured, ''You do have quite an appetite for life's simple pleasures, don't you? I understand poor little Beth Dorman feels *she's* deeply in debt to you too.''

He didn't know what that was supposed to mean. He said, ''She don't owe me. I owe her. Had not I heard her putting up a struggle out in the hallway, I might well have been the dolorous subject of that hearing this afternoon!''

Constance Farnsworth nodded, but insisted, ''Just the

same, you made quite an impression on our Miss Dorman, and she's younger and prettier than some of us."

Longarm made her blush by quietly saying, "Younger, mebbe. I'll be the judge of who'd be better-looking."

The handsome widow hastily served him more cake as she flustered, "Beth Dorman is the one who seems so smitten by you. I warned her I'd heard gossip about the famous, or notorious, Longarm. She said she didn't believe a word of it. She said she thinks you're ever so gallant and that even if you were the ladies' man some say you are, she wouldn't care."

Longarm asked if he could have more tea to go with his marble cake. She refilled his cup, demanding, "Well?"

He sighed and replied, "Well what? Are you asking if I mean to have my wicked way with a schoolmarm, ma'am?"

She nodded and confessed, red-faced, that she was.

Longarm said, "I don't set bear traps for deer mice and I don't cheat at strip poker with any gal. I'd make a play for your missing maid, or you yourself, before I'd take advantage of that poor little mouse you have running that school, no offense."

She gasped, got her breath back, and replied, "I'm not sure whether I should feel offended or not. What have my maid and I got that poor Beth Dorman lacks?"

He said, "The ability to defend yourselves, ma'am. Even you keep referring to that schoolmarm as *poor* little Beth. She wouldn't know how to say yes or no to a skunk in pants who shot sweet talk at her. It would be like taking advantage of a kid, and afterwards she'd likely bawl like one."

The widow archly demanded, "You mean you're one of those brutes who love 'em and leave 'em, as we've heard?"

He shrugged and sipped some tea before he muttered, "I

never came up here to brag on my love life, ma'am. I came to tell you what that English engineer might have told you, and I don't care whether he'd have made a play for you, your maid, or Miss Dorman. He can't, and I don't mean to. So we'll say no more about it and it's getting late. So I'd best rejoin the riffraff down the slope and see who'd like to be loved and left.''

She rose with him, eyes hurt and confused, and demanded, ''Have I said something to offend you, Custis? I was only teasing!''

He said, ''It don't matter. Like I said, I never came up here to play any sort of games, and come morning I'll be headed down your railroad with that game-playing federal prisoner. So please don't have your boys turn over any track before we can get out of here! I have seldom had such a simple mission turn out so complicated, and it serves me right for breaking the old soldier's first three general orders!''

He saw she had no idea what he meant. So he said, ''Never be first, never be last, and never, never volunteer!''

Chapter 11

A full moon was shining down on the little mountain town and somewhere a piano was tinkling pretty good as Long-arm reached the foot of the slope. He knew that couldn't be Red Robin, so he went to see who it was. It was that dismal time of a night in a strange town when a stranger just didn't know what he ought to do before bedding down and to hell with it.

The tinkling rendition of "Sweet Betsy from Pike" led him to a saloon across the way from one Red Robin had been playing at the night before. As he entered, Longarm saw the place was a tad bigger and hence seemed even emptier. He spied Oregon John and young Deputy Rothstein playing cards in a corner with four others he didn't know. An old-timer with a drinker's nose stood alone at the far end of the bar, talking to something deep in his beer scuttle. There was nobody seated at the piano as it tinkled about Betsy and her lover, Ike. It was one of those player pianos you cranked up and put a penny in. He figured that was why he hadn't heard anyone but Red Robin the night before. It made no sense to spend hard-earned pennies when a piano was playing free within earshot.

Longarm consulted his pocket watch and swore. The only gal in town he'd ever screwed was at home with her husband and fat in the bargain. Her waitress pal at the hotel, Matilda Waller, would still be on duty. He'd just told Widow Farnsworth why he didn't mean to mess with that schoolmarm. Breaking in shy spinsters was an awesome responsibility. A thoughtless night of fun with a lonesome gal who read romantic novels could lead to murder, suicide, or both.

As he bellied up to the bar and ordered straight draft just to nurse while he smoked, the barkeep asked if he was that famous lawman who'd come up their way to hunt cow thieves for Granny Boggs.

Longarm finished lighting up and replied with a weary sigh, "Not hardly. I'm only trying to get *out* of here with a federal want they have over to the jail. I understand nobody but that nice old lady has charged anybody in these parts with stealing stock."

The barkeep nodded as he slid Longarm's scuttle across the zinc to him, saying, "Ain't that many cows to steal since things have got so slow around here. With so many of the mining familes pulling out, and those left falling on harder times, there just hasn't been enough demand for prime beef to keep the smaller outfits in business. Granny Boggs and the lazy three bunch are about the last of the small stock outfits left. Everyone else has been selling off their cows and either switching to barley or leaving entire for other parts."

Longarm didn't much care. But they paid him to be nosy. So as he sipped and smoked he extracted a clearer picture of the local beef and barley situation.

It wasn't all that unusual, or interesting. He'd already been told you had to sell produce in town, to a shrinking market, or ship by rail to the outside world at less profit.

He could see why barley growers such as Colman, who he'd met aboard the train, would manage to hang on and maybe even thrive, since barley grew so easy up this way with those big breweries down in Golden paying top dollar for good barley to malt. But it seemed just as certain the stockmen up this way would be hard pressed to compete on the Eastern market with big outfits such as the Hashknife or Jingle Bob that shipped far more stock at a time from their more conveniently located spreads.

But he listened anyway, just to be polite, and the barkeep confided that one fair-sized outfit had been buying out the smaller ones with a view to the closer Denver market.

Lowering his voice as he pointed his chin at Deputy Rothstein, the barkeep said, "Lots of well-to-do folks of the Hebrew persuasion living in West Denver these days. They only eat beef butchered by some sort of Judas priest, and he'll only take prime stock, alive on the hoof, so's he can inspect 'em good before he gives them a bath and cuts their throats with an extra-clean blade. So old Jed Nolan over at the card table there with Nate Rothstein has contracted with that Judas priest in Denver for regular shipments of fat yearlings, a dozen or so head at a time."

Longarm asked casually, "By rail?" and lost interest as soon as the local man verified this suspicion. There was no way in thunder a cow thief could shove stolen stock through the town yards and aboard one or two cattle cars without someone as suspicious as old Granny Boggs taking note of the brands. In any case, stealing cows wasn't a federal offense unless you moved them (dead or alive) across a state line. So it was none of his beeswax whether, say, the Double Seven had its own proper bills of sale on every head it sold within the state of Colorado.

He was sorry he'd ordered a scuttle instead of the smaller pint-sized schooner of draft. For the barkeep seemed intent on bending his ear on such a slow night, and he didn't want to let his annoyance show, as it would he if he ran off and left his bigger glass half filled.

He was saved from having to gulp more suds than he wanted when the darkness outside was rent by a fusillade of rapid gunfire. He made it four to six shots as Deputh Rothstein sprang up from the card table, met Longarm's eyes, and cried, "Are you with me?"

Longarm allowed he was hardly *against* a fellow lawman as he tore out through the swinging doors after Rothstein, drawing his own side arm on the run.

As they ran, Longarm saw a long rectangle of lamplight spilling out across the plank walk and dusty street from the gaping door of the town constable's office and jailhouse. So he wasn't surprised to see Rothstein dash inside. But as he joined him near the rear of the front office, he was surprised as hell to see Constable Amos Payne facedown on the floor, his own gun in hand, with a neat little hole in the back of his vest and a big puddle of blood still spreading from under his mighty still form.

As Rothstein dropped to one knee by his boss, Longarm quietly told him. "He's dead. You get so's you can tell. Who's that other cuss I see still twitching yonder?"

Rothstein glanced at the other downed man, sprawled on his side on the far side of the doorway to the cell block, and replied, "That's Tim Keen, our night man here. You say they got him too?"

Longarm muttered, "Not quite," as he strode around the fallen Payne and hunkered down by the twitching and gasping kid called Tim Keen. As he did so, Longarm could see into the patent cells, and there lay Bunny McNee, spread-eagled on the cement as she stared up wide-eyed at nothing much.

Longarm marveled, "Jesus H. Christ, somebody just

95

staged the last act of *Hamlet* here with real bullets! Keep an eye on the front door, pard. I suspect they got what they came for. But you never know!''

Gently shaking the junior deputy on the floor by one shoulder, the confounded Longarm asked, "How many of 'em were there, Tim?"

Young Keen blew bloody bubbles as he mouthed what might have been: "One dirty son . . . drop on me . . . never hadda . . ." Then he just blew silently popping bubbles and stopped breathing forever.

Longarm told Rothstein, "Looks like somebody you all know came in. Our female prisoner was the target, unless she got hit in the cross fire as the killer was trying to free her."

They both rose to move closer to the cell as Longarm continued. "Whatever his intent, the killer got Keen to let him come back here to visit Miss Bunny. He wasn't expecting old Amos to step in on 'em as he was doing his dirty. Like ourselves, Amos might have heard the gunfire from outside and . . . Nope, that won't work. It was all over too sudden. So what if he had the drop on Tim Keen, Amos came in, and all hell busted loose when the killer got excited?"

By this time Rothstein had unlocked the door of Bunny McNee's cell. So they stepped inside to hunker down for a better look at her body. Longarm gingerly opened the front of her gunsmoke-stained male workshirt, whistled at the small blue hole between her cupcake tits, and decided, "Dead aim. Point-blank. Looks like the deed was done with a .45 short with intentions of silencing her. Tim Keen yonder was shot by the same sort of weapon. Unfortunately it's as common as clay. There ought to be a way to tell which sort of gun fired which brand of slug, but as yet there ain't, so we're looking for a sneaky son of a bitch of any description packing a .45-28 made by Colt, Remington, S&W, or hell, Starr!''

By this time others were crowding in out front. Longarm yelled for everyone to stay back, and muttered to Rothstein, ''The bastard could be anyone in town. Including one of *this* bunch!''

That inspired Rothstein to chase everyone but some town officials clear outside as Longarm knelt to gingerly turn the dead constable on one side. He could see at a glance old Amos had been shot in the back. Unlike the other two bodies, Payne's had been hit by a more powerful round that had blown out the front of his chest.

As that dentist who rode herd for the county coroner joined him over Payne, Longarm said, ''Looks as if there might have been two of 'em. I got a dying statement from Tim Keen yonder, and he said he only saw one. How do you like one of 'em acting as a sneaky partner for the one these two dead lawmen likely knew? Say that the visible visitor threw down on the prisoner and young Keen, but old Amos got his own gun out before the confederate blasted him from behind.''

The dentist paced the floor with his eyes closed and decided, ''Works as well that way for *me*. Amos was a tough old cuss. Shot in the back, he still managed to turn and head for the front door as both rascals ran out without closing it.''

A townsman in the crowd who'd been listening called out, ''There's what looks like a bullet gouge high over this door latch, Doc!''

So Longarm and the dentist strode over to have a look. The dentist decided, ''Fresh splinters and a streak of lead add up to a bullet to me. I told you old Amos was tough! He got off a round from his own gun with his very last breath!''

Rothstein, joining them, said, "They both did. I just looked at Tim's drawn gun too. Must have been one hell of a shootout while it lasted. Do you suppose one or more of the bastards could have been wounded in the fray?"

Longarm replied, "Can't say. Let's hope so. We could use such a break. If they got away without a scratch they could volunteer to posse up with you and go chase themselves!"

Rothstein looked blank and asked when Longarm meant to form a posse.

Longarm said, "I ain't. But if I was you, I'd surely consider it. Of course, I'd count noses and scout about for bloodstains by the dawn's early light before I led one about in circles."

Rothstein stammered, "I don't understand. I'm only a deputy constable. With poor old Amos lying there dead, wouldn't that make *you* the senior lawman in these parts?"

Longarm shook his head. "It's up to your own mayor and board of aldermen whether they want to hire someone with less seniority and put him over you. If they did that to me I'd quit. It's your own local law force that just got massacred, and that dead gal in the back was still your prisoner up until such time as your late Constable Payne could have signed her over to me. I just got here. You know the surrounding folks and country better than me. So let's not argue about jurisdiction. I got me a mess of wires to send if your Western Union is open at night!"

Chapter 12

It was. Knowing his own office in the Denver Federal Building wouldn't be, and seeing that Marshal Billy Vail would still be out of town—with any luck at all, Longarm wired Henry at his home address in hopes of saving a fellow deputy and a federal matron a fool's errand. The late Bunny McNee would keep a spell in that root cellar, with neither of those male cadavers likely to make her yell for a chaperone.

He sent more questions about the three of them to all the other logical law outfits at night-letter rates, seeing he could hardly send them collect and knowing how Billy Vail felt about spending one whole nickel a word. Night letters were sent slower and cheaper by the telegraph company during slow spells in the wee small hours when there was nothing better to send. The messages sent at night-letter rates would be delivered when Western Union got damned well ready to do so, long after old Henry was told at a nickel a word not to send anybody to John Bull after all.

By the time Longarm left the telegraph office, he saw the street lit up like a Christmas tree around the jailhouse. The shootout had been held just before country folks' bedtime, and it wasn't as if the dinky town had an opera house or one of those new roller-skating rinks. Longarm wasn't all that exhausted. But he didn't feel up to any more free lectures on basic law enforcement. So he headed back to his hotel, knowing he might face a long day in the saddle if anybody cut any sign in the morning. The annoying thing about the doctrine of posse comitatus was that every able-bodied rider was required by common law to saddle up and ride along, jurisdiction be damned. He'd left his McClellan saddle back in Denver, and he naturally didn't have a pony up this way. But he somehow felt sure Rothstein was likely to fix him up just fine. Green lawmen could be like that when they felt they could use some advice with their first big chore.

As he entered the lobby of the Elk Rack, the night clerk called him to the desk, waving a folded slip of paper as he explained how Ruby, the colored waitress at the beanery across from the jail, had left it for him around eight that evening.

Longarm reflected he'd have been up at Widow Farnsworth's around then as he took the message with a nod of thanks. He saw it was in pencil on the back of an order form from the beanery. It read:

Dear Sir:
Thank yew for sending this girl to take my supper order. I had already hurd yew wore firm but fare and I have had about enuff of this dum game. Nobody sed nothin about nobody getting kilt. Sew if yew cum too see me rite away I will tell all.
Sincere as Hell
Tess Jennings my reel name

Longarm whistled softly and confided to the night clerk, "Had not I been supping with another lady when this arrived, I might've been there when somebody meaner came calling on the late . . . whoever! You ain't the one and original Mister Cooper in charge of this hotel, are you?"

The night clerk laughed and replied, "I'd be home in bed like him if I was. Why do you ask?"

Longarm said, "Let's try it this way. In all your born days at that desk have you ever laid eyes on Bunny McNee, the kid who stayed here without paying, in broad daylight?"

The night clerk shook his graying head and answered, "Only seen him once, fleeting, in any sort of light. He checked in one noon when Mister Cooper was standing behind this desk. The hotel help says he never went out much. Even had his meals upstairs in his room and added to his bill. That's another reason he ran up such a bodacious bill. Like I said, I saw him that one time, around four or five in the morn when I was half asleep. I wondered what he might be up to at that hour. I didn't know till later he was skipping out on us. Is it true he was really a she? Just heard some others talking about it when I was sipping black coffee in the kitchen."

Longarm allowed he found a heap of things about his dead federal want confusing as hell. Then he headed next door to their dining room.

Matilda Waller was seated alone at a corner table, going over her waitress tabs while there was nobody in the place to serve. As she looked up at Longarm with an uncertain smile, he nodded curtly and told her, "I have got to talk to another waitress. If I ain't back by the time you're fixing to leave, don't leave. We might have a lot to talk about!"

As he strode out the far door to the street the waitress gasped, "After you've asked some other waitress first? I should think not, no matter *how* long Peony said it was!''

Longarm never heard that. He was moving fast in his low-heeled cavalry stovepipes. He wore boots suited to riding or walking with the weary legwork of a lawman in mind. He was starting to know the center of John Bull better than he'd ever wanted to, running around it like a confounded errand boy!

Thanks to the crowded street out front, the beanery across from the jail was still doing business. He asked the manager which of his two colored gals might be Ruby. He didn't get much cooperation until he flashed his badge and repeated his request in a firmer tone.

Ruby turned out to be the older and more motherly-looking one. She verified what the night clerk at his hotel had said about her delivering that message from the late Tess Jennings, also known as Bunny McNee. Ruby said, ''It was slow, just after most of our regulars had finished their suppers. So Mister Bob, the gent you were just fussing at, said it was all right if I ran that white gal's note over to the law. You had to feel sorry for the chile. She'd cried herself all red-eyed in that jail cell, and when she asked me to help her I couldn't say no.''

Longarm nodded soberly and said, ''I can see you have a kindly way about you, Miss Ruby. I'm sorry I wasn't there when you delivered her message. Did she tell you any more than what was on the paper, by the way?''

The motherly waitress smiled sheepishly and confessed, ''Of course I read it. It wasn't sealed up and why did you think I took time off from my counter tips to run it over to you? Mister Bob said it sounded important too.''

''The two of you discussed her message out loud behind a beanery counter, no offense?'' he asked as an alarming picture formed in his already puzzled mind.

When she confirmed his fear that any number of casual

eaters could have heard, and repeated, the contents of the dead gal's plea, he could only sigh and say, "I understand you carried earlier meals over to the jailhouse for her?"

Ruby nodded. "I thought she was a *he* until this evening. You could have knocked me over with a feather when she told me she was another gal, and in a fearful fix besides!"

Longarm explained, "*We* thought she was a he until last night. The reason I'm pressing you about this is to make sure we weren't slipped a ringer! You're certain the gal who gave you that message to me was the same person they arrested last week as a boy?"

Ruby laughed. "Now how would they ever switch any he with a she, or even a he with a he, with poor Constable Amos and his own boys watching?"

It was a good question. He said, "Let's buy them arresting what they took for a pretty deadbeat at the depot and having the same one in a windowless patent cell all this time. That's still not saying the one sneaking out of a hotel bill he just couldn't pay was the same one they arrested later, wearing the same outfit and bland baby face!"

The waitress seemed to find that an awful lot of trouble to put some innocent gal through. Longarm thanked her and headed back to the Elk Rack, a half-dozen notions juggled by his brain at once.

When he caught up with Matilda Waller again in her own less busy dining room, he glanced at the wall clock and said, "Let's scout up your boss and see if he won't let you off early. What I want with you is way more important!"

She blinked in mingled desire and dismay, then replied, "I like a man who knows what he wants and goes right after it. But Lord have mercy if this don't seem a little sudden!"

Longarm paid her no mind as he pushed through the swinging doors to the kitchen. So she followed, timidly, as

103

he found the night manager jawing over coffee with the cook and his swamper.

Longarm flashed his badge at the three of them and explained he needed their waitress to identify a dead body for the law. The gal they were talking about looked more surprised as her boss allowed he could serve any late customer they might have before closing time.

When she complained that the summer night was chill outside, he went on up with her to fetch her shawl. Like other hotel help who didn't have a good reason to rent outside quarters, Matilda Waller had a garret room up behind the false front of the Elk Rack. Longarm waited in the hall while she ducked in to fetch her plaid shawl. For some fool reason this seemed to confuse her. As they were going back down the stairs she marveled, "Do you *really* want me to go with you to some funeral parlor?"

He answered, "Nope. Widow Farnsworth sent that dead Englishman on his way embalmed in a handsome lead-lined coffin. Constable Payne and Deputy Keen will be getting tidied up for their own funerals, even as we speak. But dead riffraff due for potter's field only get to relax in a root cellar until somebody claims 'em or they start to go bad, whichever comes first."

Outside the drably pretty waitress took the arm he offered her, but protested that this was hardly her idea of an evening outing with a gentleman caller as he led her along the moonlit street. He said soothingly, "I'd be proud to buy you some ice cream afterwards, Miss Matilda. I had to dragoon you for this distasteful chore because nobody else who knew Bunny McNee as a male hotel guest was handy at this hour. I was told you carried his hotel meals up to his room. So he must have had to sign for them in front of you, in broad daylight, way more than once, right?"

She said she'd lost track of the times the deadbeat had

cheated her by adding her tip to his tab in pencil. So one got the impression she was not what might be called a friend of the dead person found in that patent cell.

When they got to the recently vacated grocery with a cool root cellar, Longarm was pleased to see Nate Rothstein had posted a night watch on the property. The junior deputy naturally knew Longarm by sight, and anxious for any distraction at that hour, said he'd be as pleased as punch to show them around down below.

He led them to the cellar stairs with a railroad lantern, and they followed him down into the dank darkness. Longarm had to help the jittery waitress on the stairs. He didn't care much for the faint but nasty odor either. It was mostly the smell of damp earth and mildew, but that first one, gunned by Amos Payne in the depot, had been dead long enough to notice. Matilda Waller pointed at the late Ginger Bancott and asked, "Didn't they say that red-haired boy had been shot? How come he looks as if somebody beat him up real mean?"

Longarm said, "They bloat and get red-faced before they get dark and start to shrivel, ma'am. Could you hold that lantern over this one they just brought in, Deputy? You'll find this one way fresher, Miss Matilda."

The late Bunny McNee or Tess Jennings only looked a mite waxen around the tip of her snub nose as she reclined on her own planks across sawhorses. Someone had been thoughtful enough to shut her eyes and place some pennies on the lids. The waitress gulped and almost sobbed, "That's him, I mean her. He, she, or it stayed up in that hired room day and night alone, save for the times Peony says he, or she, had a rougher visitor. Will I look like that when I am dead?"

Longarm said soothingly, "Probably not, ma'am. When the undertakers do right by you, your eyes and mouth stay shut by themselves and you don't stink or turn funny colors.''

He started to explain some details of the embalmer's craft, but decided not to. That friendly undertaking gal who'd explained just what they did to hold folks together long enough for a dignified send-off had doubtless been more used to dead bodies late at night.

He nudged the waitress and gently told her they could leave now. He didn't have to tell her twice. But she waited until he'd thanked the town deputy and had her headed homeward before she said, ''That was awful! Whatever made you suspect the girl killed tonight in the jailhouse might not be the boy who ran up that swamping bill at the hotel? The fact she was a girl disguised as a boy makes those visits from a rough lover more sensible than Peony put it.''

He said, ''Sense is what I'm trying to make of this whole can of worms. All three bodies answer to descriptions of wanted outlaws. But I'll be switched with snakes if I can fit the three of 'em together in a sensible pattern. Both the red-haired Ginger Bancott and the darker Quicksilver Quinn had dishonest but obvious means of support. I can see why either, riding with the sort of tomboy we just viewed, might want to keep her at a hotel instead of in the bunkhouse with the rest of the boys he wanted to fade in with. After that, it would be just plain stupid to refuse to pay her hotel tab. An owlhoot rider of any experience would have known that's no way to hide out in a small town.''

Matilda said, ''I don't think she was messing with either of those dead boys we just saw. You were right about red-headed hotel guests attracting notice, and that other one, Quinn, had *another* girl here in town.''

Longarm brightened. ''Are you sure? Might you know

this other local lady with such poor taste in men, Miss Matilda?''

To which she demurely replied, ''My friends call me Matty, and I don't known why I'm attracted to rascals either. I don't know the serving girl they say that handsome stranger in town had been seen with a lot. But her name is Sarah Something and she works for that Widow Farnsworth. Most everyone in town who doesn't work for C.C.H. seems to be working for that rich widow these days.''

Longarm said, ''I've noticed. I think I know the maid of whom you've heard gossip. She ain't there no more. Let's hope she turns up alive so I can question her about old Quicksilver. That *does* present a sort of pattern, when you study on it with your eyes half shut.''

The waitress held his arm tighter as she demanded, ''What do you want with that sassy Sarah and he hightoned ways? Was that true what Peony told me about you and her the other night?''

He said he wasn't sure what she was talking about, and was quick to explain, ''Just before they killed her to shut her up, the gal we had down as Bunny McNee told a beanery serving a supper crowd that she'd had enough and wanted out. The maid called Sarah was sparking a hired gun and working for a lady who'd hired a man murdered by a hired gun. That might add up to a *pair* of scared quail all this gunfire flushed!''

She didn't seem to follow his drift. He was still working on what it all meant in any case. So he asked if she knew a place where they might have that ice cream he'd promised her.

She laughed. ''At this hour?'' she asked, and suggested they just get on back to her place, where she just happened to have something stronger than ice cream on hand.

So they did. She said she felt no call to tell anyone they

107

were back seeing it was *almost* closing time downstairs.

Once they were up in her small neat garret room, she sat him on the bed, bolted her door, and poured something in two hotel tumblers by the moonlight through the overhead skylight. It smelled like malt liquor and tasted even better. Matty said she'd bought it for female complaints. As she cast aside her shawl and sat down beside him to clink glasses, she had to allow that a gal sleeping alone at high altitude seemed to have a heap of itchy turning and tossing to complain about.

He gravely replied he'd heard the same from some Denver ladies only a mile above sea level. As they sipped the strong stuff, they agreed that an article they'd both read about thin air made some sense. For everyone knew ladies suffering from consumptive lungs got passionate as well as wan and lovely, like that Miss Camille with all those lovers in that novel by Mister Dumas. It seemed possible that feeling breathless made a natural gal feel, well, breathless.

As she poured another round, Matty confided she'd spent many a breathless night up there behind the false front. When she sat back down closer, she breathed heady fumes in his face as she demanded, "Why did you make Peony so breathless last night, you silly?"

To which he could only reply, "It was my understanding the chambermaid of whom you speak is a happily married woman, Miss Matty."

The waitress giggled and said, "I'll bet she is. She said it made her feel really swell when you hit bottom. She said nobody had been in her that deep since she was way younger and skinnier. Did you really do that to her, you dog?"

Longarm didn't want to talk about doing it dog-style to a gal he'd never even kissed. He was mighty peeved at Peony for bragging on that with a husband waiting at home

for her. He was peeved at himself for the way it was g
him hard, just thinking about that big rump of the cheating
chambermaid moving in time with his thrusts.

He said, "I never talk about such private matters one
way or the other. Careless talk can mess up another pal's
fish story when nothing happened, or make a pal feel like
a fool when something did."

She leaned even closer and purred, "You mean if I was
to lose my head like Miss Camille you'd never tell anyone
downstairs? I ain't as coarse-natured as Peony. I could
never look another in the eyes and say right out that I'd
just kissed a bigger dick than my husband's!"

He allowed that did sound sort of coarse. And then she
was groping at his fly in a way that threatened his buttons,
so he told her he was better at undressing his fool self.
Then he rolled her in for a kiss that would have done the
breathless Camille proud as they fell flat across her matress
together. But damn if she didn't have his old organ-grinder
out of his fly by now and damn if it wasn't hard as a rock.
So without preamble or taking off as much as her dining
room apron, the breathless waitress rolled atop him, strad-
dled his fully clad form, and just hoisted her skirts to haul
the crotch of her newfangled and naughty French underdrawers aside and impale her warm wet innards on his raging erection as they both gasped deeply in that thin
mountain air.

By the time she'd bounced herself to climax that way,
she'd slipped off everything but her high-buttons, black
lisle stockings, and fake silk underdrawers. He was glad
she hadn't been wearing the kind they trimmed with black
lace. Once she'd come, she said his tweed suit felt mighty
scratchy as well. So she rolled off to coyly remove everything as he rolled upright, undressed as fast as he could,

and rejoined her in the middle of the mattress with a pillow under her bare bottom.

She gasped, "Oh, Dear Lord! You *can* plumb a girl's very depths with that tool, can't you! But Custis, dear, you do meant to keep this our only little secret, don't you?"

He kissed her, and meant it. He'd been about to ask her the same thing, and it felt swell to just let go with a sensible pal who felt the same way about good old barnyard rutting.

The frisky little gal had some barnyard suggestions of her own regarding positions she said she'd always felt curious about but had never had such a swell chance to try. Longarm found this hard to buy, but never said so as she made a liar out of her mouth with her experienced hips. The contrast between her willowy moonlit form and the far more substantial curves of old Peony the night before made a man with a curious nature of his own feel mighty fond of the both of them as he pounded away in the small garret room.

Meanwhile, out on the edge of town, a rider mounted on a lathered pony reined in to report to another rider sitting his mount in a patch of shade. "I've hunted high and I've hunted low for that nosy lawman, Boss. Lord knows where he's at tonight! He ain't in any of the back rooms along Saloon Row. He ain't with that new constable at the lockup or at home. I'd have been mighty surprised to find him with Widow Farnsworth, but I nosed about up yonder anyway. She's still up and about, drawing on maps in her dining room with that colored man in charge of her track workers."

The rider he'd addressed as his boss dryly said, "I suppose it was too big a bood to look around his infernal *hotel*?"

The man replied in an injured tone, "First place I looked. I acted innocent and asked the night clerk if he'd come in yet. When the night clerk said he had, I went next door for some coffee, waited a spell, and snuck up the service stairs like I worked there. Longarm must have thought he was too smart for this child. When I knocked, got no answer, and let myself in with my skeleton key, a match stem fell on the hall runner from where he'd jammed it in by the bottom hinge. I put it back, once I made sure the room was empty, and just locked it up natural.''

The boss swore softly. ''He's on to us. I can't for the life of me see *how*! But they warned us he was good and they warned us right! There'll be no evidence even Longarm could arrest us on before we make our final move. But it's getting to be that time, and there's no way to put things off at this late date!''

The other rider sighed and said, ''If your asking for volunteers, I ain't half the gunfighter poor old Quicksilver was, Boss.''

His boss quietly replied, ''I know. Nobody I could get on such short notice would be any better than Quicksilver, and Quicksilver wasn't fast enough to take Longarm out!''

The man asked, ''Then what are you aiming to do, Boss?''

To which the other replied, ''Take him out myself, of course. Somebody has to, and like you said . . .''

''But Boss!'' the man protested. ''Quicksilver was a professional faster than you, and Longarm still swatted him like a fly in a face-to-face fair fight!''

His boss asked quietly, ''Who said anything about a fair fight?''

Chapter 13

The traditions of the posse comitatus were rooted in old English common law on the simple notion that all the able-bodied men of the county ought to pitch in and protect common property, unless they had so much property they felt too fancy to bother.

But when Longarm, walking a tad stiff, reported to the new Constable Rothstein in the cold gray dawn, he explained he had no mount of his own and that he'd left his McClellan, Winchester, and such in his furnished digs in Denver.

Nate Rothstein didn't care. He armed Longarm with a .44-40 Winchester '73 from their gun rack, along with a box of spare rounds that would fit either his over-powered six-gun or modest borrowed carbine.

Out back, they outfitted him with the high-stepping Cayuse-Morgan cross, a buckskin mare, the late Amos Payne had ridden. So there was no graceful way of getting out of it. By the time Longarm and Nate Rothstein were mounted up out front, a good thirty others had come to ride along with their own guns and horseflesh.

As they lit out at an easy trot along the wagon trace that

at first ran in line with the railroad tracks and Mudpuppy Creek, Rothstein explained the morning train would be leaving around noon that day, because of some serious track work Widow Farnsworth had ordered. That left but one old Indian trail out of the steep-walled park. It never occurred to Longarm to say his old pal Miss Red Robin had already told him about it. He asked Nate Rothstein how you told a horse apple or hoof mark of a killer on the run from the more average cross-country rider.

Rothstein explained he'd asked around town, and determined nobody who sounded innocent had said anything about riding up over those ridges to the west since a mule train had set out a good spell before the killings at the jailhouse.

Jerking a thumb over his shoulder at a dark morose rider to their rear, Rothstein confided, "You're right about horse-shit along any trail. Old Beavertail Bill is half Ute and all tracker. He can read sign the way you and me read French novels illustrated. There's no sense trying to cut any this close to town on a well-traveled trace. But once the trail winds up through the aspen on the far side of the Double Seven, Beavertail Bill ought to be able to tell us whether anyone lit out for those newer gold fields to the Southwest within the past twelve hours or so, see?"

Longarm did. The simple plan made simple sense. He was glad they might not have to ride all the way to Holy Cross. He'd be willing to if they spotted any recent sign or, even better, blood!

A couple of miles out of town they came to where those track workers of Widow Farnsworth seemed to be following the suggestions of that Encyclopedia Britannica. The posse had to ride around the cluster of carriages drawn up along the wagon trace. The pretty Widow Farnsworth was watching her laborers from a one-horse shay she'd driven

113

down from her mansion herself. Old T.S. Nabors of C.C.H. was holding court at a sullen distance in his own coach and four, as if afraid he'd miss something the competition was up to.

As the posse rode past, Longarm dropped out long enough to tick his hat brim to the well-proportioned brunette and ask how things seemed to be going.

She dimpled up at him from under her sunbonnet and declared, "I don't know how I'll ever be able to thank you, Custis. It was all so simple as soon as you pointed it out! Half my track workers have never learned to read or write, yet they all seemed to grasp your diagram at a glance!"

Longarm allowed that was why he'd tried to draw it simple. Then he explained they were hunting for killers, ticked his hat brim again, and rode on to catch up with Nate Rothstein as he led his posse down the gentle slope toward the tracks. He naturally did so well clear of the eight-man work crew, all colored, as they sang in time while they all pried a heavy length of Wilkinson rail loose with their long crowbars.

Longarm had to rein in again. He lit a cheroot and watched with admiration as other workers grabbed hold of the loose rail with what looked like ice tongs, lifted it as one, and flipped it over like one hell of a long flapjack to clank smoothly into that long line of small steel cradles as the workers all laughed like kids. Longarm felt mighty pleased with himself as he rode on.

The feeling passed by the time he caught up with the posse again. For he didn't feel half as smart about outlaws in these parts. He didn't have an educated guess as to what in blue blazes they were up to!

He knew there had to be some around, for they kept shooting at more honest folks. But there was just no saying why. Nobody but cranky old Granny Boggs had reported any missing stock, and even her losses seemed too modest to justify any killing.

As they forded the shallow Mudpuppy Creek, there was no mystery as to where it had come by its name. At this altitude you got trout where the streams ran cold between granite boulders. You got more frogs and mudpuppies, or big fat salamanders that seldom left the water, where the streams flowed sluggishly over muddy bottoms with no shade to keep the sun from warming the water to just too cold for much swimming. The trail picked up on the far side as a narrower pair of wagon ruts. Nobody paid any mind to the fresh horse apples or cow pats they passed. Nate Rothstein had said the trail ran past the Double Seven spread.

That turned out a bigger and handsomer home spread than one expected to find up here where the grass grew greener in far smaller amounts. Someone had left a salt block just outside the cattle guard gate through the six-strand Glidden-wire fence around the main house, outbuildings, horse corral, and such. So a dozen-odd cows of various breeds and original brands lazed around in the nearby grass, as if around the cracker barrel in some bovine general store.

You could raise some of the more tender Eastern beef critters on the greener summer grass and forbs of the front ranges. So it was no great surprise to see more shorthorn stock, and even one brute who could have passed for pure Durham. Nobody had denied that Jed Nolan of the Double Seven had been buying other stock right and left to fatten up and sell as kosher beef in nearby Denver. It hardly seemed possible a big froggy in a little puddle could just help himself to the stock of smaller and likely jealous neighbors without any of them noticing, and so far not even Granny Boggs had accused this outfit of running her brand.

There was a distinct and vital difference between *running* a brand and *changing* it lawfully. When a stockman bought a beef critter fair and square, he *blotted* or crossed out its original brand without any attempt to change it. Then he slapped his own brand on to show who the critter belonged to now. By the time a cow got to the slaughterhouse it often had quite a history inscribed across its hide. That might have been why the Eastern shoe factories paid more for Argentine hides. They didn't brand beef cattle down Argentine way. Those gaucho riders just cut the balls off anyone they caught messing with their stock.

As the posse reined in out front, the burly but well-dressed Jed Nolan came out on his veranda to call in his hands and ask if anyone wanted coffee and cake.

When Nate Rothstein politely declined and told the local stockman what they had in mind, Nolan tried to sound sincere as he declared, ''I'd sure like to ride with you boys. Amos Payne was a good man, and young Keen leaves a widow to mourn for his life. But you see, I'm all gussied up to ride into Denver, where I have to catch me a Chicago train. I hope to be back by the end of the month. But I ain't coming back before I get a good price on at least one of those fancy refrigerated railroad cars such as Armour ships his butchered and trimmed beef to market in.''

Someone in the posse called out, ''Them Chicago ice boxes on wheels are built broad-gauge, Jed! How in thunder do you expect to get one up all them miles of narrow gauge from Golden?''

Nolan smiled smugly and replied, ''That's for me to know and you to find out. We live in changing times and I paid for *my* education. So I don't aim to pay for anyone else's.''

Nate Rothstein laughed and said they'd best ride on. By this time a pouty-looking redhead in a mint-green summer frock had joined Nolan and the others out front. Nobody laughed when the obviously rich son of a bitch introduced the stunning young thing as his woman. Most of the locals already knew her, though not as well as most men would have wanted to. She seemed put out that nobody would come inside and even taste her swell chocolate layer cake. When Rothstein repeated they'd best get going, the older stockman turned to a younger and taller cuss wearing a red shirt and chinked chaps cut off just below the knee, and suggested he gather some of the other hands and ride with the posse.

So he did. As they all made it back to the westbound trail, a single-file rut through the grass by then, Rothstein introduced the red shirt to Longarm as Buck Lewis, the ramrod of the Double Seven.

Longarm filed and forgot the names of the four other cowhands the big boss had sent along. Buck Lewis seemed neither elated nor depressed by what was shaping up to be an all-day ride. When Beavertail showed some interest in a fresh horse apple swarming with bluebottles, the foreman laughed easily and called out, "That's be Casey or Old Dick, scouting for a lion we heard pestering the stock the other night. I sent them after the son of a bitch with some redbone lion dogs this very morning."

Longarm asked how far Lewis figured his own hands might ride after a stock-raiding lion. When the ramrod figured no further than the next ridge west, Longarm casually asked whether that mule team bound for Holy Cross had passed by the spread back yonder.

It didn't make him feel any better when Buck Lewis confirmed a handsome brunette had been riding in the party with a gambling man or that Red Robin had gotten along just swell with everyone save for Miss Amanda, the owner's young wife. Longarm wasn't surprised to hear Red

Robin hadn't cottoned to a genuine redhead after all the trouble she'd had to go to with henna dye and bleaching potion.

The trail got steeper and wound over some slickrock. Longarm's borrowed buckskin made it to the far side, then commenced to limp like hell. So he reined in, dismounted, and lifted what seemed to be the offending hoof between his tweed-clad knees, muttering, "Aw, shit!"

Young Rothstein wheeled his paint to ride back and ask what was the matter.

Longarm explained, "She's cast a shoe, Lord knows where, and now she's split her hoof on that son of a bitching slickrock! You'd best ride on. This mare ain't going nowheres. I'll lead her back down on foot and they might be able to fix us up at the Double Seven."

Buck Lewis, who'd ridden back to join them, called out, "Tell 'em I said to. We got a well-founded forge out back, and our Mexican smith knows his job no matter how he talks."

Longarm thanked the ramrod for the information, and led the hurt pony to one side until all the others had passed by them on the narrow trail.

Once he had the gimpy mare back across the slickrock she was more willing to walk with him. He let her set her own pace and even brouse some aspen leaves along the way. For he knew he'd hate like hell to walk barefoot with the callus split to the quick.

So it took them a spell. But as all things good or bad must end, they got the crippled critter back down to the Double Seven. Once Longarm had asked him politely in Spanish, the skinny old Mexican farrier said he'd be proud to staple her split hoof and reshoe her.

As the older Mexican and his young helper got to work on the mare out back, the redheaded Amanda Nolan called

Longarm inside from her back door. It would have been rude to snub the owners as he availed himself of their forge and hired help. So he strode on over and took off his hat as she led him inside for some of that chocolate layer cake.

They had it in the kitchen, served by her Indian cook, of course. He wasn't surprised to find the cake oversweet. The lovely but not too bright-looking Amanda seemed surprised when he declined her kind offer of canned milk and lump sugar for his coffee.

Seated across the pine table from him, the redhead said he'd just missed her husband. It appeared Old Jed, as she described him, had ridden into town early to attend some business before catching his train.

When Longarm remarked that the train would be leaving later than usual that day, she said they'd heard, and added, "Business, business, business, morning, noon, and night! That's all Old Jed is interested in, and I swear he won't be satisfied until he owns all of Colorado and has me knitting socks in an insane asylum!"

Longarm refused to even nibble at the bait. It sure beat all how pretty young gals turned down honest work or simple young men in favor of rich old farts, and then complained that their husbands were rich old farts.

It wasn't easy, but he managed not to comment on her big fancy kitchen range and such being bought and paid for by a man who spent more time at business than, say, strumming a guitar or reciting poems to her. He wasn't totally unsympathetic to her plight. He knew he'd never in this world be rich as J.P. Morgan, or even Old Jed, unless he learned to drive himself with a whip and never waste time wondering about things like why roses were red and violets were blue instead of the other way around. But fair was fair and he couldn't fault a man who only thought about business, as long as his business was within the limits of federal law.

He washed down some cake and casually asked the scatterbrained redhead if she knew how her husband meant to find a narrow-gauge refrigerated car. He explained, "Most of those mountain railroads are short-line, meant to just carry ore and produce down to where it can be loaded on regular rolling stock. It ain't for me to say, but I'm sure it would be simpler to ship livestock at least as far down as Golden, slaughter 'em there, and send the trimmed sides to market in regular refrigerated cars you could buy or, heck, rent off the broad-gauge by the shipment."

She just looked blank. He explained, "You folks may be big by the local standards, Miss Amanda. But not even your husband could raise enough beef up this way to get that serious. Gents who talk business more than we do call it 'economy of numbers' because the way you sell produce changes as you change the amounts."

She looked stunningly stupified.

He insisted, "You take the Colmans, growing barley up the line a piece. Barley grows good up here where it's well watered and cooler. Those big breweries down Golden way will likely buy all the barley Colman cares to grow for 'em, so's they can turn it into barley malt and mix it with hops someone else grew to make lager beer for the big Denver market. But Colman just can't grow enough barley on his homestead claim to justify his own processing. He's better off selling his grain fresh from the combine and letting *them* worry about all that processing, see?"

He could tell she didn't. He still said, "The butchertowns over Chicago way, Omaha way, and even Denver process more cows in a day than all you stockfolk up this way could ship 'em a year! They run 'em in single file to be sledged, hoisted, bled, and drawn almost as fast as I can say it. The neighboring plants along Butchertown Row process every part of the cow but the moo, from horn, hide, and bonemeal to disgusting leftovers I'd as soon not mention in front of you ladies. You can make a pretty penny processing pure trash, if you have enough of it in one place. But setting up a butchertown up at this end of that narrow-gauge? I just don't know, Miss Amanda.''

The redhead simpered and said, ''There's a *lot* you don't know.''

So their Indian cook murmured, ''Miss Amanda!'' in a desperately quiet tone.

But her mistress said, ''Pooh, he's a lawman and there's nothing unlawful about moving this whole shebang up to Wyoming Territory, where the grass grows fair-green on the prairie and you don't have to wait forever for the durned train!''

The older Indian gal sighed and said, ''Just the same, we were told it was to be a family secret until the time came, Miss Amanda.''

The redhead shrugged and smiled as shrewdly as she knew how at Longarm, saying, ''You won't tell anyone like Granny Boggs, will you? I do go on in front of company, and Ute Mary is right. We weren't to tell anyone.''

Longarm assured them both he only had to report federal offenses he might come across. Then he politely declined a second slice of cake, polished off his black coffee, and excused himself to see how they were doing with his borrowed mare.

The old Mexican and his young helper had done her proud. She barely limped at all when they led her around out in front of the forge. So he thanked the farrier, asked what he might owe, and insisted on leaving at least a fistful of cheroots when the older gent refused any *dinero*.

He was still riding her at a walk on soft ground when,

just west of Mudpuppy Creek, he met up with another town deputy, headed the other way on a lathered bay. The younger lawman said, "It's awful! How far up this trail might Nate and the others be?"

Longarm said, "No more than two hours ahead of you at the rate you're riding. What's so awful, old son?"

The deputy tersely replied, "French Sarah, the stuck-up maid who worked for Widow Farnsworth. They dumped a whole tram of ore atop her in the hopper of the stamping mill before they noticed her frilly white petticoat and naked thigh. She'd have really wound up awful if they'd tossed her in whilst the mill was processing ore! The assistant coroner and undertaking druggist agree she must have been strangled last night and tossed in that ore hopper like a rag doll nobody wanted no more."

Longarm said, "They could be guessing closer than they really tried. Her boss lady noticed she was missing yesterday afternoon. Before that, she'd been seen in the company of the late Quicksilver Quinn."

The deputy marveled, "Kee-rist, she was sparking with that gunslick you had it out with at the school?"

Longarm nodded grimly. "The same. I'd say she heard her lover had been killed, went to his pals for consolation or mayhaps a train ticket out of here, and like the dentist and druggist suggested, they had no further use for her!"

The young deputy gulped and said, "She'd have never been found if the mill crew hadn't spotted her in their hopper before they had a head of steam up in their boiler. I know she was stuck up, but wasn't that a mighty shitty way to treat any woman?"

Longarm allowed it seemed a shitty way to treat anybody, and the deputy rode on to catch up with the posse as Longarm continued his slower ride back to town.

As he forded Mudpuppy Creek again he stared ahead,

and saw that track crew and all those carriages he'd seen on the wagon trace beyond were gone. Hearing one of her help had been murdered had likely unsettled Widow Farnsworth a mite. So he and his gimpy mount had the wagon trace to themselves, or thought they had, as they moved up the grassy slope at a walk, taking little notice of the close-growing and fluttering aspen on the far side.

It was just as well Longarm was a kindly rider. For had not he noticed the far shorter but far steeper berm of the wagon trace and reined in to gracefully and suddenly dismount, that rifle spanging up amid those gray-green aspen trunks might have blown him backwards over the cantle of his borrowed stock saddle.

It had surely been *aimed* his way!

The pony, unmindful of his intent to lead it up on the roadway on foot, simply spooked at the noise and lit out for the familiar smell and security of its stall in town, dragging its reins and going like blazes despite having to favor its off-front hoof.

By this time Longarm had landed in the grass on one shoulder and rolled as he drew his six-gun, cursing that fool buckskin for running off with that Winchester.

But at least he had plenty of ammunition in one pocket of his tweed outfit. So he cranked off the five he'd been packing in the wheel through the dust thrown up by his bolting mount. Then he flattened behind the berm and rolled some more as somebody returned a heap of shots through the cloud of gunsmoke he'd just offered them as another target.

He reloaded, popped up again, just high enough to blaze away blind as he spied other gunsmoke drifting among the aspens, and then ducked down to crawl in the opposite direction while reloading along the way.

Hence his unseen enemy wasn't expecting to spot him

in that direction as Longarm sprang to his long legs and made it across the wagon trace in a half-dozen running strides, crabbing to one side as he got in among the skinny but closely packed trunks before someone got to peel some smooth bark where a more direct approach might have taken Longarm.

So Longarm fired back a lot, and was rewarded by the yipe of a kicked dog, or a terrified man, as his damned .44-40 ran down some more.

Longarm zigzagged the other way as he moved in on the sound, braced for more return fire as he reloaded in the deep shade of the fluttering green and silver leaves of the nearly solid canopy above. But there came no more return fire, and it surely sounded like someone else was plowing off through the grove without half as much caution.

Longarm kept moving in slow and silent, aware of many a crow bird being taken in by one hunter leaving while another lagged behind.

Then, off in the distance north of the grove, he heard the sound of hoofbeats lighting out as if some rider had just had the shit scared out of him.

Longarm chuckled, but moved on cautiously until he came to a patch of trampled forest duff, a handful of smoked-down cigar stubs, and something else.

He bent over to pick up a cigar ring and the high heel of some frightened soul's Texas boot. He could see at a glance how a two-hundred-grain .44-40 slug had blown it out from under the cuss with a lucky shot. He had to grin as he pictured the startled expression on the rascal's face when he'd yelped like that.

Longarm moved on and found another spot where the already spooked rifleman had tried to make a second stand, spilled some spent brass, and lit out running after yet another lucky shot had thunked into an aspen trunk above his fool head.

Longarm pocketed some of the brass. Most everybody loaded saddle guns with the same handy .44-40 rounds, unless they were after bigger game than, say, a deer, a lion, or a man. But not everyone bought the same brand. So now he was looking for a son of a bitch who puffed on Gallo Claro cigars, wore those new Justin brand boots, but favored cheap P&P ammunition.

Chapter 14

Longarm got back to town the hard way, asked around until he made certain that the buckskin and all the other public property had made it safely without him, and went over to the Western Union for some more discussion of recent events with the outside world.

As he'd hoped, there were already some answering wires waiting for him. But as he tore each open he only became more puzzled. Nobody else in the game of catching crooks had been able to connect either Ginger Bancott or Quick-silver Quinn with Bunny McNee's gang, and more than one seemed surprised as all get-out to learn Bunny McNee had been a gal.

Longarm picked up a pad of yellow telegram forms and proceeded to wire his home office that he'd been wrong the last time he'd wired. For whatever in blue blazes was going on surely had to be federal. He had no idea what they were up to. But anyone moving so sneaky and sly had to be smart enough to know it was serious.

He wasn't ready to say for certain whether he or the late Gaylord Stanwyk had been Ginger Bancott's intended victim. But he knew for a fact they'd sent Quicksilver Quinn and somebody else more recently to gun him in particular!

Outside once more, striding along the walk, he spied the sign of a cobbler with an Italian name. He didn't go in or even glance inside as he passed. He could ask somewhere else whether that was the best, or only, place to have a boot heel replaced. Meanwhile, it was a mite early to worry about that. The rascal he'd spooked back there amid those aspen had most likely gone to ground here in town, to wait and see how warm his intended target was before coming out to play some more.

At the jailhouse they told him Widow Farnsworth had paid the town druggist-undertaker to tidy up and embalm her dead maid so she could be shipped home to her kin in New Orleans. They were fixing to convene a coroner's jury just after supper time so it would be all right to seal the swell coffin a generous employer was springing for.

Longarm headed for the Farnsworth mansion up the slope. There had to be some reason they'd killed such a pretty little thing. She'd have had to know something they didn't want anyone else to know. The secret couldn't have been that she'd had rotten taste in men. A heap of folks in town had known she'd been playing slap and tickle with the late Quicksilver Quinn. His pals would have had no good reason to worry about her going to the very lawman who'd killed her lover for a nice long chat.

That same snooty butler let him in, took away his hat, and allowed he'd see if Madame was receiving on such short notice.

Constance Farnsworth was. She was wearing a shantung house robe and an unsettled expression as the older colored gent led him in to her smaller sewing room. She wasn't seated at her fancy Singer machine. She was perched on a nearby window seat, with her feet in satin mules and drawn up on the cushions with her, as if she felt like a child left home alone with darkness coming on.

In point of fact it was barely noon outside. That late train of hers hadn't left the roundhouse yet. Getting right to the point, he asked her if she could hold off sending it down her line until Nate Rothstein and that posse got back.

She nodded and reached for a bell pull as she soberly asked, "Do you expect the monster who killed poor Sarah to make a run for it aboard my Golden-bound combination?"

He said, "Can't say yet. What I thought I'd ask your new constable to try might or might not flush some unusual birds."

That butler came in. She told him to send a footman over to the roundhouse and tell them she'd send further word when and if she ever wanted that Shay locomotive to move again.

When they were alone some more Longarm explained. "I know for a fact that Jed Nolan told his wife he was headed down your line on a serious business trip. Right about now he'll be starting to pace the floor of your waiting room. There'll be others with sensible reasons to ride down to Golden on a workday. There might be some who seem to be leaving town unexpected. We can sort them all out once we let the train leave, stop it in open country a mile or so down the park, and see just who might be aboard."

She said she followed his drift. Then she swung her slippers to the rug, patted the seat cushions where they'd been, and bade him sit down and tell her how he'd ever gotten so smart.

Longarm remained standing as he modestly allowed, "I've been at the same puzzle-solving chores for six or eight years now, riding for the law. You get to where some pieces look familiar, since there are only so many ways a crook can move."

She asked why he didn't want to sit down beside her.

He said, "It ain't what I want, ma'am. It's what there's time to do in the time I have to work with. I got to move on now. I only stopped here to ask you to hold that train."

She smiled up wistfully. "Consider it stopped until you send word you want it to move. You will come back and tell me what on earth's been going on, promise?"

He smiled back as wistfully and said, "I'll be proud to, as soon as there's more time and I have the least notion what I'm talking about!"

He left her there and prowled back through her house to the kitchen, where he found that old frog-faced butler seated grandly at a table, having his cake and coffee served by a skinny young gal of a similar complexion.

The butler rose stiffly to say, "It is customary to ring when you desire something from the staff, suh."

Longarm said, "I ain't back here as a guest. I'm back here as the law. I heard Miss Constance call you Edward. If you'd rather I call you Mister I'll need a last name."

The butler stiffly replied that Edward would do fine, and added he knew nothing about the murder of that sassy Miss Sarah, save that he'd told the pretty Creole gal not to mess with that Texas trash they'd called Quicksilver.

Longarm nodded gravely and declared, "She should have listened. What I wanted to ask of you would be more in the way of an introduction. I've noticed more than a dozen colored folk up this way, and it's been my experience that there's usually a colored quarter tucked in some corner of a town this size."

The butler and the colored scullery maid exchanged wary glances. Edward shrugged and said, "There's no secret about that. Me and the other household help sleep up under the mansard shingles. The mostly colored railroaders are housed in company cottages on the far side of the roundhouse. Some other colored families here in this tight little town have naturally built or hired other quarters next to the railroaders, on railroad property. Miss Constance don't mind. Her husband treated us decent while he was alive, and she's carried on as a white boss of quality.''

Longarm nodded and said, "I don't have time to convince you my folks were too poor to keep slaves in days of yore. Your boss lady, her railroad, and a heap of track-working jobs could be in danger. I need your help to mayhaps head some off. Do I have it?"

Edward nodded gravely, but asked, "What can I do? I just work here.''

Longarm included the young scullery maid as he explained, or verified, what they'd likely noticed already.

He said, "You colored folks tend to be either annoying or invisible to a heap of white folks. When you ain't getting shot by brutes such as Clay Allison for ordering a drink in a white saloon, you tend to be tolerated, and ignored, as faithful darkies waiting on tables, shining shoes, or whatever.''

Edward quietly asked if Longarm was trying to be funny.

Longarm assured him, "Not funny. Factual. I've noticed in connection with other federal cases that white bullies tend to go on talking as if they were alone while colored help is quietly serving them. I've noticed that next to barbers, nobody gossips more, in low tones, about the scandalous or just plain silly things the white folks in town may be up to than their colored help.''

The scullery maid was grinning ear to ear. Edward sternly warned her not to get uppity, but confided to Longarm, "She caught that New Orleans gal doing it in the woodshed with that Quicksilver man one evening. But we ain't about to gossip like that about Miss Constance!"

Longarm said, "I ain't interested in what a lady might

do in her own woodshed. I want to talk to someone privy to *all* the gossip of all you invisible folks. Before you ask me what I want to know, if I knew all that much I wouldn't have to ask. I have a whole bunch of balls in the air with no basket to put 'em in. If only I could connect or disconnect my obvious suspects . . .''

"You want to talk to Mammy Palaver, the Obeah woman," Edward said. The scullery maid nodded, with a wicked grin.

Longarm smiled less certainly and asked, "Obeah? Ain't that somelike voodoo?"

Edward said, "Voodoo is a religion. Obeah is serious. Even our good Baptist ladies go to Mammy Palaver for goofer dust or just good advice. So she would naturally hear a lot."

Longarm nodded thankfully, and asked how he might find this witch woman and whether he should say Edward sent him.

The frog-faced but dignified gentleman of color gravely told him to just ask when he got to the colored quarter. Then he added, "You won't have to tell Mammy Palaver who you are. She'll know. All of us heard a powerful lawman was coming our way. It was Mammy Palaver who spread the word you were all right. Your point about white gunfighters gunning our boys for no good reason was well taken. So we watch you all more than you might think."

Longarm said that was the very point he'd been trying to make, and left by way of the back door.

He'd already been told French Sarah was over at the undertaker's, and he figured the dentist and druggist who examined more dead folks than he did knew when a gal had been strangled or shot. So he headed up to the mining operation to examine the scene of the crime.

He walked as far as a barbed-wire fence and a posted

gate, where a shotgun-toting C.C.H. man told him all the property beyond was his outfit's private property, damn it.

Longarm flashed his federal badge and explained he'd come friendly for a look around that ore-stamping mill, or else he'd be back directly with a search warrant and an armed mob. So the guard let him through, and even pointed the way to where they'd found that dead gal.

Longarm would have found the stamping mill in any case. It was three stories high, sending up a lot of coal smoke, and making a dreadful racket near the tracks running through the dusty confusion of tipples, sheds, and such between him and the mine adit set in the bare side of a mineral-rich young mountain.

He found a dusty denim-clad work crew running pulverized and high-graded ore into an open gondola car the same gauge as Widow Farnsworth's little railroad. A lot more worthless spoil was being piled up, and up, between the stamping mill and a head rill of Mudpuppy Creek. If they didn't want a little lead with their mud, it was tough shit as far as C.C.H. cared. Old T.S. Nabors would likely declare he shipped as much of it as possible to the smelters down in Golden.

Once he'd read Longarm's identification papers and figured what he wanted, above the ear-splitting thunder of the steam-powered ore-crushing machinery, the straw boss led Longarm to a nearby office shed, where they could hear one another better behind the closed door.

The straw boss poured them a couple of snorts from a bottle filed under B for Bourbon and told the sad tale of French Sarah about the way Longarm had already heard it.

He was able to explain why the killer or killers had been forced to dump her body where it had been found in time after all. Sipping his own whiskey, the mining man said they'd been working short daylight shifts and added, "Nobody could have ever climbed the open stairs with a body if the mill had been manned and running."

Longarm said he'd already figured that, and asked if a killer with a knack for mining machinery could have started the mill up, with or without permission, once he'd dropped the poor gal in the hopper up above.

The straw boss pursed his lips and decided, "It'd be possible but tough. We naturally leave a banked bed of coals under the boiler all the time. Takes hours to start a steam engine up from stone cold. But I doubt there'd have been enough steam up to run her and that ore she lays on through the mill. Not without poking and stoking the fire-box and waiting for a good head of steam, leastways."

Longarm tried to picture the scene. It was not a pretty picture no matter how you drew it. He said, "They might have been anxious to leave. They could have slipped both ways through that three-strand fence in the dark, whether the gate was guarded or not."

The straw boss said, "Some other lawmen scouted for sign along that pesky fence. We never needed one when we were mining high-grade for real gents instead of rag-pickers. They found nothing to say how that dead gal came on the property, dead or alive."

That notion painted a *really* ugly picture. Longarm reached in a pocket as he said, "We only know of one local gent she'd been seeing and he'd have been dead when she left the Farnsworth mansion to see someone else."

He produced the boot heel and cigar band, asking, "Can you think of anyone with business on this site who smokes this brand of cigars or stomps around a mining operation in cowboy boots?"

The straw boss shook his head, observing, "I know them claros from Cuba cost more than this child can afford. The big boss, Tough Shit Nabors, smokes Havana Perfectos. I'd say your claro smoker pampers himself a mite, whether he can afford to or not. Claros are mighty mild as well as too expensive for an honest workingman.''

He added he'd never seen anyone mining hardrock in cowboy boots, but that some of the company police thought they were Wild Bill in the flesh. Longarm had been afraid he'd say something like that. It left *that* ball way in the middle of the air.

He figured asking company police in high-heeled boots whether they'd just been shooting at him in an aspen grove might be a waste of time. So he handed the straw boss a cheroot in exchange for the drink and they parted friendly.

He could see the tin roof of that railroad roundhouse down the slope from the C.C.H. tracks. So he strode down along them, noting in passing how easy it would have been to walk or carry French Sarah up to the stamping mill by that unguarded route.

He found the whitewashed company cottages and some extra tarpaper shanties near the roundhouse, where old Edward had said he might. A couple of colored kids were playing mumbly-peg in the dirt with a jackknife. When he asked the way to Mammy Palaver's, one ran away, but the other pointed at a slot between two cottages and warned him the Obeah woman might turn him into a horny toad or gopher snake.

Longarm allowed he'd take his chances, and strode over to find the apparent gap beween whitewashed cottages was the entrance to a sort of smoke-filled cavern, improvised from scrap lumber and flattened out coal-oil cans. The smoke smelled more like smoldering herbs than firewood. As he hesitated in the low overhang, a cheerful voice called out, ''Well, don't just stand there, child. Come on in and tell Mammy what you want her to make better!''

He went on back to where he could barely make out a

once pretty and still friendly-looking colored lady dressed in a white cotton smock, with a purple head cloth and a whole lot of small bones and big beads strung as a triple necklace. She was smoking a long pale cigar. When Longarm started to identify himself she laughed, took the cigar from her lips, and said, "I knew you were coming to John Bull before you got here. I told the chillun how you saved that colored rail-yard man from a mighty ugly bunch of hobo boys that time. I'm telling you now, ain't none of us colored folk been up to no good in these parts!"

Longarm gravely nodded and declared all the suspects on his list so far seemed to be white folks. He asked if she knew Ute Mary over at the Double Seven, adding he'd just been by there and that the cook had tried to shut her mistress up.

Mammy Palaver said, "Ute Mary been to see me for some love potion. Ain't no Indian medicine men left in these parts. She ain't the one who wants to hide her romance with Buck Lewis, the white foreman down that way. *He's* the one who's ashamed to take an full-blood gal to dances in town. I told her she didn't need no potion for that white boy. He ain't been fooling with the other gals on that spread, because all but Miss Amanda are true to their husbands, and Miss Amanda thinks she's too high-toned for raggedy hired help."

She took a drag on her cigar and added, "She's right. Ain't got a peck of brains in her pretty head, but Buck Lewis ain't good enough for Ute Mary. That stingy old Jed Nolan only pays a foreman top-hand wages and a half. Do they move that beef operation out of here, like some say, Ute Mary won't have to worry about her Buck Lewis. He'll be lucky if they take him to Wyoming with them, and Lord knows they'll never be dragging Indian kitchen help that far!"

135

Longarm didn't ask why. Depending on how full-blooded she might be, Ute Mary was lucky they hadn't already moved her on out to Utah Territory with the rest of her North Ute kin. The Bureau of Indian Affairs would frown even harder on her winding up on recent Lakota and North Cheyenne range. In their Shining Times the playful young men of those nations had described the North Ute as their favorite enemies. The Ute had counted coup on them many times as well.

Longarm cautiously asked if Mammy Palaver had any notion who Amanda Nolan might be fooling with on the side. The Obeah woman declared she knew for a fact that the redhead had spent a night at the hotel with one of those mining men the last time her husband had been out of town on business. Longarm perked up as he got out his notebook. But then she had to spoil it all by declaring the redhead's adulterous stay at the Elk Rack had been well before that confusing Bunny McNee had run that hotel tab up.

As long as he had his pad and pencil out, he questioned Mammy Palaver about all the other slap and tickle she'd heard about up this way.

An Obeah woman who sold love potions heard a lot. The tiny town commenced to sound like Sodom and Gomorrah with Zeboiim and Nero's Rome thrown in. He was more saddened than shocked to hear poor old Constable Payne had been coming from a tryst with a married woman on the night of his death, and he didn't want to hear about the late Deputy Keen and that colored waitress across the street.

He was a tad disappointed to learn Tough Shit Nabors seemed to be content with his own young wife. They both agreed rich old men seemed to attract the better-looking play-pretties.

Mammy Palaver had kind words to say for Constance Farnsworth as well. She allowed the pretty young widow

136

was either still in mourning for her man or mighty discreet. Then she spoiled that by adding with a shrug, "That uppity Edward would never tell anyone if he caught her in bed with President Hayes and Jesse James at the same time. But listen, have I told you yet about that minister's spinster daughter who loves her dear daddy more than the Good Book tells her to?"

Longarm shook his head and murmured, "Don't have any ministers on my list of suspects. Do you mind if I ask where you might have gotten that swell Gallo Claro cigar?"

She calmly allowed a client had bought a box for her, and named the one fancy tobacco shop in town that carried the brand. He asked if her client had been a white cowboy in Justin boots. She found that a droll suggestion, and explained that the colored foreman of that track-working crew had needed some goofer dust to use on a love rival.

Longarm doubted a man of any race would rely on both folk magic and P&P .44-40s to deal with anyone he wanted dead. So he thanked the kindly old witch and went on back to the center of town.

As he approached the jailhouse he saw heaps of pony rumps and assumed that posse had come back. He learned he was right when he strode in to be told Constable Rothstein had just gone over to the undertakers for a look-see at that dead gal.

Longarm went after the younger lawman, and caught up with him in the cellar of the drugstore, where the druggist ran his sideline as the town's only and hopefully occasional mortician.

He'd thought French Sarah had been nicely built when she'd served him with no more than tea and pastry at the Farnsworth mansion. When one considered what her petite body had been through since then, it was surprising, and distressing, to see how tempting her pale naked flesh looked as it lay on that cold table with the undertaking druggist powdering her dead nose.

Nate Rothstein turned from watching to nod at Longarm and declare, "Small blood flecks in her eyes and only the bruises around her windpipe, despite the drop and a sudden stop on chunks of ore. They tell me we can save the county some bother and her kin some distress if we list the cause of death as strangulation at the hands of a person or persons unknown."

Longarm nodded soberly and agreed. "She lit out from her job at Widow Farnsworth's early in the day, as soon as she'd heard her boyfriend had lost a gunfight with yours truly. She might have demanded they send somebody else after me. She might have demanded money to get out of here before anyone could tell me she'd been out in the woodshed with a wanted killer. In either event, the one she went to killed her on the spot, waited until dark, and then carried her up to that stamping mill to get rid of her."

He stared wistfully down at the dead gal and asked if the posse had found any sign further west. He wasn't surprised to hear they hadn't.

Longarm nodded and said, "I have a plan that might tell us more, whether anyone makes a break for it by rail or not."

He explained what he'd worked out with the pretty owner of the narrow-gauge. Rothstein said it sounded good to him. So they went on up and out to the street, where Rothstein yelled for a kid he knew to go tell Widow Farnsworth to let her combination head down to the outside world in, say, half an hour.

Then the two of them legged it back to the jailhouse, gathering posse members from saloons along the way, and then, mounted on yet another borrowed pony, Longarm led them the same way they'd ridden before.

As they rode, Buck Lewis caught up with Longarm to ask where they were headed and why. When Longarm tersely told him they were fixing to stop the train where that westbound trail left the wagon trace, the Double Seven ramrod laughed and allowed he'd meant to be home for his supper in any case. Longarm didn't ask whether he preferred to have it served by a naked lady in bed. Mammy Palaver had said he was a tad embarrassed about being a squaw man.

A heap of old boys were. Kit Carson and William Bent had married up properly and lived openly with Indian wives. But more often it was hidden as if it was a secret vice. Old boys who thought nothing of being seen coming out of a whorehouse, whooping drunk, would gun you for asking what they'd been up to in that tipi the other night.

He had time to consider that angle as they lined up across the tracks near that shallow stretch of Mudpuppy Creek. But there was just no way anyone with a lick of sense would want to gun a federal deputy to keep a secret widely known by local gossips. It was simply sad but true that a rider drawing even a ramrod's pay was never going to do much better than a drab white gal or the sort of pretty Ute Mary. It wouldn't be a federal crime if old Buck *could* get at his boss man's prettier dimwit.

The Shay locomotive came puffing down their way and, since the engine crew had been warned they'd be stopped a few miles out, they braked the combination smooth as silk to an unscheduled stop as Longarm and Constable Rothstein swung aboard from their ponies, guns drawn, to ask some questions.

The handful of startled passengers had questions of their own to ask. Old Jed Nolan was mad as a wet hen, having been delayed in town for hours, only to be stopped again a few minutes after getting on his goddamn way to Chicago!

Longarm soothed him with a few words about the murdered maid. Nolan allowed he and all these other folks had already heard about the goddamn murder and had to be on their goddamn way.

It didn't take long to determine Nolan was goddamn right. All his fellow passengers could produce tickets bought with no indecent haste, they all had sensible reasons for wanting to run down to Golden or Denver, and not a one of the sons of bitches made a lick of sense as a suspect.

So they let the combination go on its way, with apologies. As it puffed on south, Buck Lewis and the three Double Seven riders with him wanted to know if they were still possed up.

When Longarm and the new constable allowed they were fresh out of ideas, Buck Lewis laughed boyishly and said he'd been planning on an early supper after all that riding.

It wasn't easy, but Longarm managed not to mutter, "Kiss her once for me!" as the four of them splashed across the creek for home.

Nate Rothstein asked, "What do we do now, Longarm?"

It was a good question.

Chapter 15

That one cobbler back in John Bull agreed with Longarm that he'd surely shot the heel off someone's Justin boot. You could tell because it was produced by Joseph Justin in Old Spanish Fort, down Texas way, to standard machine-carved patterns.

The old goat-faced cobbler was the one who pointed out how dumb it would be to have a heel replaced by the only cobbler for miles a few minutes after losing it in a shootout with the law. He said if he'd ever done a thing like that, he'd just get rid of the shot-up boots and put on a new pair.

His words made a heap of sense. Levi jeans, Stetson hats, and Justin boots had gotten common as clay, in that order, between the '40s and '70s, because each product was well made at affordable prices for the average rider. A few pair of boots would be far less expensive, in the end, than getting caught in the older pair by a federal lawman.

Longarm asked the canny cobbler how many places in John Bull might fix a jasper up with new Justins on short notice.

The cobbler shrugged and replied, ''Aside from myself? There'd be the saddle shop, the general store and a couple of haberdashers who deck a gent out from head to toe. Why does he have to replace his old pair with the same brand? Have you considered he might have had more than one pair at home to begin with?''

Longarm groaned aloud and said, ''This is what I get for asking an expert on shoe leather! Can you tell from that heel what size boot the rascal takes at least?''

The cobbler shook his head and answered, ''No. That's one reason Joe Justin can sell fair boots at store-bought prices. He makes no more than a half-dozen sizes with Goodyear welts on lasts of average width. He bangs on a lot of pre-cut standardized parts. I doubt he needs more than three heel sizes. This one's medium, meaning your mysterious friend wears anything from a man's size seven to a twelve.''

Longarm muttered, ''Well, shit, I figured he was walking about on natural-looking *feet*. But I thank you just the same.''

He went next to the fancy tobacco shop near the hotel to show them the cigar ring he'd picked up out in the woods. They sold lots of Gallo Claros from down Cuba way by the box or for two bits apiece. They told him everyone who was anybody bought fine cigars to hand out while announcing births, engagements, or a good business deal. Mild claro cigars were safer to hand out than, say, Parodi Brand, which cost almost as much and upset the womenfolk when you lit one up indoors.

Longarm got out his notebook and explained the situation before he read off his list of suspects or, hell, potential witnesses. But he drew another joker from a mighty tedious deck. Nobody he could name had bought Gallo Claros direct, though anyone might have given anyone else a fistful, intentionally or not, at any number of recent social affairs. That was the trouble with changing times. There were all sorts of real-estate closings, new partnerships, and such to be celebrated. Or mourned. A businessman who got the better of you in a deal had to show he was a sport by offering you a drink or a smoke.

Longarm allowed that as long as he was taking up their time he'd stock up on his own three-for-a-nickel cheroots. They told him they'd throw in a Gallo Claro if he wanted to spring for a dollar's worth.

It was tempting. That Cuban cigar Mammy Palaver had been smoking had smelled swell. But his far cheaper cheroots were as bad a habit as he could afford on his wages. So he wistfully declined their kind offer.

It got worse as he was leaving with two bits worth of cheroots. They warned him it would cost way more if he changed his mind and bought a Gallo Claro in any saloon.

As he strode away he reflected on that. Having made a habit of buying his tobacco sober, he'd forgotten how most saloons stocked up on high-priced cigars to be sold at a handsome profit to big spenders after a few rounds.

So that meant he was looking for someone he couldn't describe, in new or spare boots, smoking a brand he could buy, or be given, most anywhere. That was assuming he hadn't been given or bought another brand since!

Longarm told himself to quit running in circles, and made a beeline for the Western Union. Once there, he found more answering wires that didn't seem to answer much, along with a to-the-point-indeed message from his home office. Marshal Billy Vail was back, and not at all pleased to hear that Bunny McNee had been a gal or that the team he'd sent to fetch whatever had been had been replaced by whatever Western Union had deleted. The late Mister Ezra Cornell had instructed his Western Union crews not to send anything worse than "son of a bitch" over his wires.

Longarm got the impression he was supposed to head on

back to Denver as soon as possible. The federal want he'd never been sent to fetch was dead. None of the other tales of blood and slaughter sounded like federal offenses, and nobody from Denver seemed to have any notion what it had all been about in any case.

Longarm had to agree his superior's fussing made some sense. The great unwashed was always raising hell in places like John Bull. That was why they had their own damned lawmen. The Justice Department simply didn't have the manpower to tame every tiny town.

He wired his boss that he'd heard and would obey. Then he stepped out on the walk, aware there'd be no train out for well over twelve hours, and wondering what he was going to say if old Peony and Matilda both showed up at his hotel room after dark.

A shorter gent in a stovepipe hat stomped up to him and demanded in an imperious voice what he meant to do about the murder of that maid from the Farnsworth mansion.

Longarm had to think before he recalled the face and name. The imperious grump was Justice of the Peace Silas Hall, and he had to be so grumpy because it was an election year.

As if he'd read Longarm's mind the J.P. said, "I just came from a sit-down at the Republican Club. Everyone from the mayor to junior alderman agrees we'll all be out of a job come November if all those blamed murderers remain free among the voters of this township! It was bad enough with the mine changing hands and business going to hell in a hack. So don't you think it's about time you made some effort to earn your pay, Deputy Long?"

Longarm smiled thinly and replied, "Been trying, above and beyond what they pay me to try, your honor. I see by some wires I sent that you never paid Amos Payne or any of your lawmen half as much as they pay me, and I have to smoke three-for-a-nickel cheroots. If you people don't think Nate Rothstein is any good, how come you promoted him to constable, aside from getting him so cheap, I mean?''

The J.P. changed the subject by saying he'd been headed up to the town hall for the latest coroner's hearing. He asked if Longarm meant to appear before the panel again.

Longarm shrugged and replied, ''If anyone asks me. I don't know a thing about the death of French Sarah that most of the folk in these parts haven't already guessed. Only her killer or killers know any more for certain.''

They walked up to the town hall together anyway. This time the crowd was even bigger. It was if they were all trying to keep up with a magazine serial by Ned Buntline.

He saw all the folks he'd ridden up with from Golden aboard that train the other day. Pretty young Flora Munro sent her kid brother, Joel, to see if Longarm wanted to sit with them inside. But he said he had to respectfully decline. He didn't say it was because Widow Farnsworth had just shown up in her one-horse shay. He followed the J.P. inside before they could all get in trouble.

The same dentist was presiding with a somewhat different panel for this one. The dead gal's body was across town, being packed for shipment to New Orleans. But everyone had already agreed on the cause of death. *Who'd* caused it was the mystery.

Longarm took a seat near the front and listened with all the interest he could muster as witness after witness was called to confess they had no idea who'd killed French Sarah. None of the servants at the widow's place had seen her leave. They'd just noticed as the day wore on that she didn't seem to be there any more.

Widow Farnsworth was asked to take the witness chair and, to his credit, that dentist asked sharp questions. Con-

145

stance Farnsworth was as sharp, or innocent. She explained she had indeed replaced Sarah on short notice because she'd planned on receiving a guest to a formal supper that evening. Longarm was just as glad they never asked her who.

Another panel member asked what she'd have done if the missing maid had come home to serve supper with a good excuse.

Without batting an eye the lady who ran a railroad and a heap of other stuff replied, "I'd have given her two weeks' pay in lieu of notice and sent her on her way, of course. There's no excuse for walking off the job in the middle of the day without telling a soul where or why you're going."

There came a murmur of agreement from the crowd. Someone behind Longarm said, "I've been told she treats all her help fair and pays her track workers the same as they'd get if they was white."

The dentist asked her if she had any reasons to suspect her wayward servant had some new swain, since her established lover, the late Quicksilver Quinn, couldn't have strangled her in some fit of passion.

The young widow sniffed and replied, "Good heavens, we'd only just heard about Mister Quinn! Naturally I'd been told she'd been seeing that ruffian on her own time. But on reflection, I thought it best not to let her know I knew."

The panel agreed that sounded fair, and dismissed the widow as a witness. As she turned to rise, her eyes met Longarm's and she smiled wanly and silently mouthed, "Supper at seven?" as she passed him.

He had no way to answer. Then they were asking him to come on over and have a seat in front of them. So he did.

He failed to see why. It only took him a few moments to assure them he'd barely known the late French Sarah and had no idea how she'd wound up strangled in that stamping mill.

The dentist insisted, "We heard someone pegged a shot at you as you rode back from Jed Nolan's spead this morning."

Longarm shrugged and said, "It was more than one shot, and I'd split off from Constable Rothstein's posse with a lamed pony. I thought this hearing was to determine who might have strangled a lady, not who pegged a few shots at this child."

The dentist allowed, not unreasonably, they could be talking about the same person or persons unknown. He asked, "Doesn't it seem that Englishman, Amos Payne, Tim Keen, and that maid were killed to keep them from talking to you, Deputy Long?"

Longarm shook his head and replied, "All four of 'em had plenty of chances to talk to me before they were killed. I don't have one sensible thing to tell myself and they keep trying to kill *me*, don't they?"

The dentist insisted, "Mad dogs don't hire professional killers, and there's no argument about what both Ginger Bancott and Quicksilver Quinn were. So how do you connect those two?"

Longarm flatly replied, "I can't. Neither can anyone else, no matter where I wire. Like the late Bunny McNee, Bancott and Quinn had piles of warrants out on 'em. But never in connection with the same crime. It's as if a mixed bag of owlhoot riders, hearing things were confusing in a tiny town with a mighty modest law force, showed up separately."

"Only to join forces when they met or somebody hired them," the dentist proclaimed.

It hadn't been a question. But Longarm answered it, saying, "If it works out that simple I'll buy you a good cigar. We know Ginger Bancott was sent to kill that Englishman before he could tell Widow Farnsworth how to run her railroad. Then Amos Payne killed Bancott, and so it couldn't have been *him* who killed Payne, Deputy Keen, and a female prisoner who might have been acting as a ringer for the real Bunny McNee. Everywhere I've wired has McNee down as sort of a soft boy, not a real gal."

The dentist nodded and said, "The killings at the jailhouse had to be the work of Quicksilver Quinn. Then he came after you at the school and—"

"Rein in and back up!" Longarm cut in. "How could one killer have shot three victims with two different guns? Or assuming a two-gun man, or one .45 loaded willy-nilly with longs and shorts, why would he then go after me? I hadn't said I knew who'd killed my federal want along with your town law. I was fixing to leave town. I'd have been *gone* by this time had they let me. We agreed about this time yesterday that Quicksilver Quinn was never going after anybody again. He was dead before poor little Sarah vanished. I don't see how he could have tried to drygulch me earlier today either."

When they went over it all another tedious time, and agreed it seemed impossible to put any of this recent wild behavior together in a sensible pattern, the dentist declared Miss Sarah DuVal, as French Sarah had been more formally known, had met her death when some unknown son of a bitch had choked the life out of her. Then he banged his gavel and allowed it was over for now.

As Longarm lit a fresh smoke outside, he noted the sun was just fixing to go down behind the mountains to the west. Most of the folks in town had naturally had their suppers before heading over to the hearing. So it was getting to be that lazy, all too short time of the day they called gloaming, when the older folks rocked out on the porch swings and the kids played kick the can as the cool shade of evening spread across their play before bedtime.

A female voice from behind him whispered, "You will drop by our place for at least some coffee and cake, won't you?"

He quietly replied, "Maybe later. I know you fashionable folk eat late. But I ain't sure I can make it before, say, eight or nine."

Then he saw he'd been talking like a fool to Flora Munro instead of the older gal who'd already invited him to a late supper.

He stared all about till he saw the back of Constance Farnsworth's shay driving off. So he couldn't even tell her he might be tied up in town for a spell.

Young Flora was blushing in the gloaming light as she dimpled up at him and said, "Why, Deputy Long, whatever gave you the notion I'd invited you to supper? Can't you see it's after seven o'clock at night? I just thought you might like to drop by on your way home and, well, meet my mom and dad."

He gulped and managed not to let his horror show as he quietly asked if her folks didn't milk cows a ways outside of town.

When she said their spread was an easy walk if he didn't have a pony, Longarm laughed and said that while he'd be proud to walk ten miles to meet such a pretty gal's mom, he had to help their Constable Rothstein track down the rascals they'd been talking about inside. So the pretty young thing flounced off to where her kid brother was holding their buckboard for her, and Longarm strode on through the gathering shadows.

Two little girls were playing jacks on the porch steps as

he went by a mustard-colored cottage with a lamp already lit behind lace curtains. It was that hour in the day when a tumbleweed gent got sort of tempted to quit tumbling and put down some roots.

But a couple of houses up some shrew was shrilling at her man through their own lamp-lit curtains about it being time he got off his lazy rump and found a better-paying job. So then Longarm remembered why he'd held off this long on settling down.

It was sad but all too true that they called that first month a honeymoon because that was about as long as the sweetest gal could hope to stay sweet. In his time he'd met many a gal who'd seemed a combination of Cleopatra and Little Bo Peep, only to wake up in bed one morning with the Witch of Endor. When you thought about it, old Cleopatra had nagged Marc Antony into trying for a better job and winding up in an early grave.

He had fonder memories of loving gals, such as good old Roping Sally up Montana way, who'd died before they could get used to his screwing and start wondering why he didn't hit Billy Vail for a decent raise.

The only gals who never nagged him about the way he carried on were gals who seemed to carry on the same way. Sometimes they served to remind him why other gals might fuss at a man for his natural ways. He knew he had no right in this world to feel miffed about Red Robin heading over to Holy Cross with some other horny son of a bitch he just hated to picture in certain positions with her. But he was honest enough with himself to know that pissed him off. Fair or unfair, there was something bred deep in the bones of men that made them want to hog all the gals in their cave and bash in the heads of any other male brutes who messed with them.

He paused in mid-stride to ask a telegraph pole beside

the walk, "Say, pole, do you reckon we ought to look into that married woman poor old Amos Payne had been messing with on the side?"

The pole didn't answer. It still saved Longarm's life when what sounded like a big metal hornet went buzzing through the space his natural stride would have carried him to if he hadn't paused in mid-stride that way. The muzzle blast of that first rifle shot caught up with the buzzing as Longarm dove headfirst over a picket fence to wind up in a weed-grown yard on his rump, gun in hand, as he tried to figure where that rifle shot had come from. The echoes off the walls all about would have made it tough enough without all those townsfolk running outside to yell back and forth over their yard fences. The old lady who owned the weeds he was sitting in came out to call Longarm a fool kid, and then something worse when she spied a grown man acting that silly on her property.

One of Rothstein's kid deputies tore up the walk, gun in hand, to ask what was up. Longarm rose, his own gun down at his side, to tell the old lady he was sorry and tell the local lawman he didn't know, adding, "Somebody just pegged another shot at me. As you can see, he missed."

From her porch the old lady wailed, "There ain't supposed to be no gunfire within the city limits. Come November my man is voting Democrat! There's been way too much gunfire in John Bull of late!"

As Longarm stepped back out on the walk, they were joined by the new Constable Rothstein himself. Nate had heard enough as he'd come running to declare, "This is getting serious as hell, Longarm. Who do you figure it could have been?"

Longarm looked disgusted and asked, "How would you like that, alphabetical or numerical? I just walked away from a public hearing in your town hall. So just about anyone in or about your fool town could have watched me walk away and noticed what a tempting target my back made!''

He made a sweeping gesture with his gun muzzle as he added, ''Here comes half of 'em now. Whoever fired on me from betwixt or from inside any houses in sight could have hidden his damned rifle and circled around to come over and ask me who I thought it was!''

Rothstein scowled and demanded, ''See here, are you accusing anyone I know?''

To which Longarm could only reply, ''Don't get your bowels in an uproar. I never said it was you. Albeit I wouldn't be surprised to learn it was some two-faced prick we both know!''

Chapter 16

Old Edward let him in and took his hat, but made him wait alone in the parlor for a long time before Constance Farnsworth came in in a Turkish bathrobe, glowing as if she'd just stepped out of her bath, to tell him he was early and ask him if he minded waiting no more than, say, half an hour for that supper.

As he rose politely to his feet, Longarm told her he couldn't wait half a minute. He explained, "I just come by because I never got to tell you at the town hall I'd be too busy this evening, ma'am. I got orders to leave for Denver on your morning combination, and meanwhile, someone keeps shooting at me. That makes me dangerous company for any lady to sup with, and I'd sure like to know why. So from here, I aim to to talk to another lady about a possible motive for at least one out of five killings. I don't see how that Englishman, a gal pretending to be a sissy boy, Deputy Keen, or your poor maid Sarah could have shot Amos Payne for fooling with their wives. Neither Stanwyk nor Keen have ever been connected with any married gals in John Bull, and those two dead gals have even better excuses. Old Amos didn't. So I have to see if I can find out who the married gal he was fooling with might have been.''

The local widow took his sleeve to sit him down beside her as she said, ''I can tell you. From time to time I have tea in the kitchen with Mammy Palaver. She gathers mighty fine herbs for some . . . female complaints, and you're not the only one who enjoys gossip.''

He grinned sheepishly and replied, ''When we do it it's called investigation. Another nice lady I know once told me I had a swell job to go with my nosy nature and authoritarian disposition.''

Widow Farnsworth arched a brow to ask, ''Oh? Just how nice to you was this younger girl who found you so dominant, Custis?''

He didn't tell her about another widow, a tad older than her, down Denver way. They all seemed sure any other woman in a man's life had to be younger and prettier.

He said, ''We were talking about more important gals. You say you know who the late Constable Payne might have been messing with?''

The pretty young widow shrugged her bare damp shoulders inside her fluffy robe and replied, ''There was no might about it, according to the darkies. Prunella Thalman, the druggist's spoiled wife, carried on with others as well, with her servants serving them refreshments in bed!''

Longarm whistled and asked, ''Are we talking about the druggist who runs that undertaking business in his cellar?''

She nodded. ''Karl Thalman. He took care of my poor Frank after that sudden heart stroke two years ago. That's why I was sure poor Sarah was in good hands.''

Longarm grimaced and said, ''So was Amos Payne, when his lover gal's husband got to embalm him the other night! I'd as soon not talk about all that prodding and poking even a friendly undertaker has to do, seeing we're all going to go through such treatment some day if we're lucky enough to get buried decent.''

She blushed a mite as she murmured she could imagine what a less friendly undertaker could do with that big suction pump to the lover of his wife.

When he asked if the colored help thought the boss man knew what was going on under his own roof while he was at work, Constance told him she didn't know. So he said he meant to go find out.

She followed him out to the foyer where his hat still hung. As he reached for it she shyly touched his sleeve again and pleaded with him to come back and tell her as soon as he knew anything.

He smiled wistfully down at her, hat in hand, and said, ''There's no saying how late that might be, if I find out anything. Whether I do or don't, I hope you understand I have to get it on back to Denver in the morning.''

She sighed. ''You told me. That doesn't give us much time, does it? I'll be waiting here, Custis, for as long as it takes, or until that damned train leaves in the cruel sunlight of reason!''

So he took her in his arms and kissed her. It seemed the only way to say so long, and she bumped and ground hello as she kissed him back. But he still busted loose and headed back down the slope. For she'd been right in more ways than one when she'd said they didn't have too much time.

The drugstore was closed and shuttered for the night when Longarm got there. But he saw light from the cellar window to one side. So he circled around for the cellar entrance. They'd told him Thalman had to get that dead gal packed right for her long lonesome journey home.

But when he hunkered down by that barred window, he saw Sarah DuVal was not the body old Karl Thalman was working on with his pants down. The nice coffin Constance

Farnsworth had paid for was across the cellar on a pair of sawhorses. The body on the embalming table was alive as well as naked as a jay. She seemed to be a colored gal in her teens who could move like she'd been at it for years.

Longarm stood up, strode on to the cellar entrance, and lit a smoke to give them time to settle down a mite. He'd finished his long cheroot and was thinking about some discreet knocking when he heard some laughing from below and stepped clear as the sloping cellar doors popped open and the druggist cum undertaker helped the colored gal up the steps with a grab at her ass that made her giggle some more.

Then they spotted Longarm and froze in place, as if embarrassed, even though they'd both put their duds back on.

Longarm nodded casually and said, "Evening, Mister Thalman. I was just now coming to see if you were through with that French Sarah."

Thalman tried to look professional as he stiffly replied that he and his assistant, Emma Lou, had just finished.

Longarm knew that was true. He took a deep breath, let half of it out so his voice would sound neither too high or too low, and said, "That's swell. Is there any way just the two of us could have a few words in private, Mister Thalman? What I wanted to talk to you about ain't for any young lady's delicate ears."

Thalman gulped, told the pretty colored gal to run on home alone, and suggested the saloon catty-corner across the street out front.

As they headed across, the stars were winking on up above, and it was a good thing there was going to be a full moon rising any minute. For there were no street lamps and the light from the few places still open made for mighty tricky lighting.

Thalman tried to hold out, but halfway across he stopped

to blurt out, "Is it about Constable Payne and my Prunella?"

Longarm glanced around at the shifting inky shadows up and down the dusty street and quietly replied, "We'll talk about it over in that saloon you suggested. I like to have my back to a wall when I ask delicate questions of any grown man."

Chapter 17

As seemed usual in the once booming John Bull, business seemed as slow as hell in the dinky hole-in-the-wall establishment the druggist across the street had suggested. One old cuss with a drinker's nose was holding up the bar with his belly as they entered. But as Longarm and the druggist took a table against the back wall, the old-timer staggered past them through a beaded curtain, allowing he had to take a leak out back.

The barkeep came around one end of the fake mahogany to greet Karl Thalman as the regular he likely was. Longarm said they'd have the usual. As the barkeep went back to fetch whatever they were fixing to have, Karl Thalman stared soberly at Longarm and said, "They told you my Prunella fucks around. They told you true. Prunella would fuck a snake if somebody would hold its head down for her. I can't tell you whether she'd been carrying on like that with either of those dead gunslicks. It wouldn't have surprised me, though. Over the years I've caught her with total strangers from, say, fourteen to forty. She doesn't like 'em much younger or older than that. She says it takes a grown man's dong moving with childish passion to satisfy her soul."

Longarm said he'd read an article by some alienist in Vienna who said gals like that were driven by a desperate itch no mortal man could ever quite satisfy, so they had to keep trying.

Thalman nodded gravely and said, "Certain drugs help. That's why despite all her wild ways she's never really wanted to leave me."

The barkeep came back with two shandies, half lemonade and half beer. Longarm thought that was a waste of either, but he'd said they'd have Thalman's usual, so he had to be a sport.

As they found themselves speaking in private some more, Longarm asked Thalman, "You mean you don't *want* her to leave you, despite what you say she is?"

The skinny middle-aged man sighed and replied, "Did I tell you she was built like a Greek statue, had a pussy as tight as a schoolboy's ass, and never, ever gets tired of moving it just right? She only fools with other men because she just can't ever get enough. On the other hand, any man married to a freak like my Prunella gets all he wants and then some, any time he wants it. She never invites any of her lovers to the house after I get off work."

Longarm could see why Thalman liked lemonade in his beer. Talking about his wayward wife left a nasty taste even when it wasn't your woman you were talking about that way.

Longarm spied two familiar figures entering the dinky saloon as he asked Thalman soberly, "Then you only had Amos Payne down as one of many?"

Old Oregon John and Buck Lewis, the ramrod from the Double Seven, nodded at Longarm as they bellied up to the bar. Thalman's back was turned to them as he replied, "Amos and me were pals. He knew I knew. The two of us had shared other pussy in town in our day."

"Like that, ah, assistant you were with just now?" Long-arm had to ask.

Thalman never blinked as he nodded and replied, "Her too. But you should have seen the big Irish gal who left here with her own husband a few weeks ago. Six feet tall with red hair all over and she liked to get on top. As for our colored help, I don't see why I shouldn't screw some of them. Prunella sure likes to!"

Longarm said, "I follow your drift about your unusual marriage. Would you like to tell me where you were early this morning and, say, ninety minutes ago when I was coming out of the town hall?"

The older man thought, shrugged, and said, "This morning I was filling prescriptions and applying makeup to that dead girl in my cellar. You have to lay on just a little color at a time and let it dry or they wind up looking like dead dance-hall gals. As for ninety minutes ago . . . I think you'll want to talk to Emma Lou Brown about that."

Longarm said he'd take his word he'd been screwing in his cellar, figuring how long such a session usually took from start to finish.

So Thalman finished his shandy, they shook on it, and he got up to leave. As he did so the younger Buck Lewis invited Longarm to join them at the bar.

Longarm did so, sliding his own shandy across the sheet copper and asking the barkeep if he could have a regular beer. As the barkeep turned to do so, Longarm held off asking what Buck was doing back in town or why he'd exchanged his red shirt for a dark blue one. Longarm's back teeth were suddenly floating and he said so, adding, "I didn't know I had to piss this bad before I stood up just now. The crapper's in the back, right?"

The barkeep said, "Way back. Across the yard. Try not to wet the seat."

Longarm said he'd watch his aim, and ambled back toward that beaded curtain. Buck Lewis and his older companion exchanged glances and shoved away from the bar as if to tag after him.

It might have worked. But as Longarm approached the bead-veiled exit to darkness a stray current of air wafted the odor of a Gallo Claro cigar his way.

He knew neither he, Karl Thalman, nor the two behind him had lit any sort of cigar in recent memory, so he threw himself to one side and dropped between two empty tables as all hell busted loose.

As the barkeep would say he saw it later, Buck Lewis and Oregon John had just drawn, thrown down on Longarm's back and opened up when that double-barreled Greener ten-gauge poked through the beaded curtain to blast Buck Lewis and spin him around like a ballet dancer doing a dance of the dying swan, while the second awesome discharge blew old Oregon John clean out on the walk through the stained glass next to the usual exit!

Then Longarm was back on his feet to dash over and kick Buck's fallen six-gun the length of the brass rail along the bottom of the bar before he dashed the other way, through the swaying strung beads, to throw down on a familiar figure sprawled by his shotgun in a spanking new pair of Justin boots.

It was young Will Posner, who'd said he rode for the Lazy Three and hadn't wanted Longarm messing with his true love, Flora Munro.

Longarm hunkered down and gingerly opened the front of the love-struck cowboy's shot-up gray shirt. The kid was still breathing. It was tough to fathom how. Longarm said, not unkindly, "You keep playing with guns and sooner or later someone's bound to get hurt, sonny. I know that was you in them aspens earlier. Where's the rifle you had the last time we met down by the town hall?''

Posner croaked, ''You bounce around too unsteady for a rifle, you sweet-talking cuss! I heard you talking sweet to my Flora some more this evening. So I figured this old Greener and some number-nine shot was just what it would take to make you quit!''

''Asshole!'' Longarm muttered as he made sure the jealous idiot had no other gun and relieved of him of his extra ten-gauge shells.

He went back into the tap room to see it filling up with others. One of them being Nate Rothstein, he yelled, ''Constable, you'd best send some men out to the Double Seven in force. Tell 'em to arrest all the help and bring Miss Amanda Nolan into town with them so's she can wait safely for her husband at the hotel.''

But then the dying man at their feet croaked, ''Hold on, boys. I don't want you arresting Uto Mary or good old Valdez. They don't know nothing. Oregon John said he'd never trust a Mex. So we never invited the bunch at the smithee to join, and as for good old Mary, I was only sleeping with her. I was too smart to trust any woman with a serious secret.''

Longarm holstered his .44-40 and hunkered down beside Buck Lewis to remark conversationally, ''I heard about them highwaymen getting betrayed by false-hearted women. Irish track workers like to sing songs about 'em. Oregon John was your *segundo,* right?''

Lewis croaked, ''He knew all the trails across these mountains as good as most Indians, and we didn't want to ask Beavertail Bill if he wanted to join the venture.''

The new town constable had drifted over by those beads to look through them and gasp, ''My God, you shot Will Posner off the Lazy Three too, Longarm?''

Longarm replied, simply, ''I never got the chance. Both

162

sides got one another as they worked at cross-purposes to get *me*. Now hesh and let me get the details out of this one while there's time. It won't matter whether Posner lives or dies. He was just an asshole with nothing important to say.''

Turning back to Buck Lewis, Longarm got out his notebook and pencil stub. ''Tell me who was in and who was out, if you don't want everyone on the Double Seven spread hauled in.''

Nate Rothstein rejoined them, saying ''Posner's gone. That makes it two out of three, and how come this one's still with us?''

Longarm growled, ''They filled Will Posner with slugs whilst he was peppering them with buckshot. It ain't any bitty ball in particular that does you in. The effects of all them perforations accumulate. Now hesh and pay attention whilst old Buck here gives us some names.''

The internally bleeding ramrod of the Double Seven began to reel off names Rothstein said he knew. Buck Lewis stopped at eight and said that was it. Rothstein said he'd posse up again and get out to the Double Seven after them before they lit out.

But Longarm said, ''Let 'em. The innocent men and women on the spread will be safer once they're gone. You can beat 'em to either Golden or Holy Cross by Western Union. They'll have to make for one or the other without Oregon John to lead them through rougher country.''

Karl Thalman, the druggist, came in and announced, ''I heard. Nothing can be done for Oregon John out on the walk. Is that Buck Lewis you shot this time, Longarm?''

The federal man snorted in disgust and said, ''Never mind who shot whom. I want him to keep talking while he can. Go over to your drugstore and fetch us some laudanum and strychnine tonic.''

The druggist whistled and asked whether Longarm meant to make old Buck dopey or pep hell out of him.

Longarm replied, "Whatever it takes. Get going."

Then he turned back to the shot-up Lewis, gently observing, "They say confession is good for the soul. So before your soul has a mighty serious discussion with Saint Peter, be a sport and tell us how Ginger Bancott and Quicksilver Quinn fit in."

Lewis croaked, "Quicksilver was up our way on the dodge from the law. He was looking for a job to tide him over. So he naturally came to me at the Double Seven for one. I could see right off he was the sort of jasper me and Oregon John were looking for. So I let him in on our plans and the rest you know. I don't know anything about that Ginger Bancott who shot that Englishman. He wasn't working for us. Mebbe the other bunch as shot up the jailhouse?"

Rothstein called him a pure rascal and insisted, "Come on. Are you trying to tell us that wasn't you or someone you sent who killed Constable Payne, poor Tim Keen, and that he-she back in that patent cell?"

Lewis insisted that was about the size of it. His voice was getting weaker. The barkeep came over with a shot glass of brandy. Longarm took it from him, drank the contents in one gulp, and said, "Thanks. I needed that."

Rothstein insisted, "Make him tell us why they gunned that gal in pants and my pals. Damn his eyes!"

Longarm said, "Hesh. He just now said he didn't know anything about that." Then he poked Buck's bloody blue shirtfront, saying, "We know you killed French Sarah. Which one of you raped her first?"

The dying man blinked owlishly and gasped, "Nobody raped anybody! I had to strangle her when she showed up out by the spread, fussing at me to kill you for killing

Quicksilver. I never treated her with no disrespect, though. She'd been Quicksilver's girl! What sort of a shit-heel would screw a pal's woman?''

As if he'd been paged, Karl Thalman came back in with a basket of patent medicines and a roll of gauze. As he hunkered down beside them he quietly asked, ''Which do you want to give him first? Neither one is going to save him, you know.''

Longarm nodded soberly and said, ''We'll just start with soothing laudanum. He don't seem to be holding out on us and we may as well make him comfortable.''

So Thalman uncorked the opium-alcohol tincture and put it to the ramrod's now ashen lips. Buck swallowed a good slug, coughed up some bloody slime, and softly said, ''No shit, am I really fixing to die?''

Longarm said, ''Yep. That cowboy surely cleaned your plow with his old Greener. But if it's any consolation you nailed him good, even if you *were* aiming at my back.''

Buck Lewis smiled up innocently and softly asked, ''What part of you did you *expect* this child to aim at after you'd taken Quicksilver Quinn? It wasn't nothing personal, Longarm. We'd have had no call to gun you if we hadn't seen you were on to us. How the blue blazes did you ever get on to us anyway?''

Nate Rothstein loudly demanded, ''How did who get on to what? Why didn't you tell the rest of us if you knew what they were up to all the time, dad blast it!''

Longarm said, ''I didn't know shit until just now. This poor misguided youth was a victim of his own guilty conscience. I did tell everyone I'd come up your way to transport Bunny McNee back to the Denver District Court. When I never did any such thing, they added two and two to get twenty-two. I've done that myself in my time.''

Rothstein said, ''I can see old Buck here was the mastermind. I can see why he wanted you and Constable Payne out of his way. But I still don't see what he was masterminding!''

Longarm gave the ramrod another sip of laudanum. He'd noticed in war that dying men made less of a fuss about it if you got them doped up and drunk. As he did so he told Rothstein, "The notion of a criminal mastermind is a contradiction in terms. Nobody with a lick of sense takes up crime as his chosen career. You just heard him confess to choking a woman to death. So I'm taking him at his word when he says he never sent Ginger Bancott to gun that Englishman and had nothing to do with the shooting fray at your jailhouse the other night.''

Rothstein groaned, "Oh, shit, thanks for making things seem so simple! Could I at least have a hint as to what on earth this one and his bunch were up to?''

Longarm answered simply, "Stealing stock, of course. What would you expect a ramrod and a gang of top hands to steal, shithouses?''

There came a confused rumble from the others standing all around. Rothtein said, "Nobody at this end of the park has suffered all that many stock losses, no matter what Granny Boggs says!''

A man in the crowd wearing silver-mounted spurs chimed in. "Nate's right. Where would anyone hide that much stock around here if he did steal it? Are you trying to tell us this dying rascal has a stolen herd up some side canyon, and killed folks to keep his purloined beef a secret?''

Before Longarm could answer, Buck Lewis plucked at the tail of his tweed frock coat and croaked, "I ain't ready to meet up with Saint Pete, Longarm. Can't you do something for me? I feel so cold and can't we have more light in here?''

166

Rothstein murmured, "Give him some strychnine! He's fading fast and we haven't got the half of it out of him yet!"

Longarm shook his head and softly replied, "I reckon he's told us as much as he knew. Nobody can deny him his lethal intent, but the only one they really murdered was French Sarah. Whether the county can nail anyone but her confessed killer on murder in the first or not ought to depend on how well they try to make friends with your district attorney. But I'm sure he'll tell them that."

Buck Lewis murmured, "Whee, this merry-go-round is sure going faster now. They warned us you were good, and it was a pleasure doing business with you, Longarm. No hard feelings?"

Longarm quietly replied, "I reckon not. The two-faced little gal *was* trying to get us *both* killed. Say hello to French Sarah when you meet up with her in Hell, old pard."

Buck Lewis didn't answer. Longarm reached down to shut his blank eyes as he told the druggist cum undertaker, "He's all yours now."

Rothstein tamped a boot heel like a gal waiting overlong for her carriage ride and snapped, "Damn it, Longarm!"

So Longarm got to his feet, saying, "I could use another brandy. Haven't you figured the whole thing out yet? No offense, but you're fixing to make a piss-poor lawman if you have to be led step by step by one hand."

The well-spurred stockman slammed on the bar for a round of hard liquor and said, "I'm forty-eight years old this summer and you can just lead me by one hand all you like, Denver boy! You say all this fussing and feuding was over stolen stock, and I say to you nobody in these parts has had any damned stock *stolen!*"

Longarm explained, "That's because Buck and his boys

hadn't stolen any yet. Their boss, Jed Nolan, was planning on moving his operation up to Wyoming and expanding it some. I doubt old Jed meant to raise anyone's wages. he wasn't paying top dollar, and mayhaps old Buck there didn't want to work that hard for *any* wages. So they were waiting for Jed Nolan to leave Buck in charge of his spread and all his stock while he went clean over to Chicago on a long-planned business trip.''

The stockman who'd been saying he was so puzzled suddenly let out a trail whoop and declared, ''Great balls of fire! I see it all now! That's where Oregon John fits in! I know Jed Nolan planned on a two-week business trip. He told me so just the other day. So not a soul would know all them Double Seven cows were on their way over the mountains before their lawful owner got back!''

Someone asked, ''What about Miss Amanda, Jed's wife? Ain't she still out at their spread and wouldn't she notice if they commenced to round up and drive off all her man's stock?''

Another local laughed and asked, ''How? That mail-order play-pretty wouldn't know a cow was being stolen if they ran it through her bedroom whilst she was reading one of her romantic novels from back East.''

Rothstein soberly pointed out, ''Buck could have meant to kill her the way he killed that housemaid. We just heard him admit to being rough on women.''

Longarm nodded, but said, ''It's a moot question how many folks he *meant* to kill as he went into the cattle business for himself. The only deaths that lead direct to his door are those of French Sarah and that fool cowboy in the back. Quicksilver and Oregon John were on *his* side, and you could almost say Will Posner's death just now was accidental.''

Rothstein blinked owlishy and replied, ''The hell you

say! Who do you suspect of killing that Englishman and three others at the jailhouse if it wasn't that dead rascal or one of his sidekicks?''

Longarm knocked back his second free shot before he declared in a firm way, ''It's beyond suspicion into almost certain. My boss calls it process of eliminating. You peel away suspects who couldn't have done it, and unlikely ways things could have happened, until you get to where there's nothing left to peel away and then you look at what you have left.''

Rothstein was shifting from one foot to the other like a kid who had to take a piss as he almost bawled, ''Then what have we got left?''

Longarm stared wondrously at the greener lawman and demanded of him, ''Lord have mercy, don't you see it yet?''

Then he spelled it out, swept the curious crowd thoughtfully with his gun-muzzle-gray eyes, and declared, ''We'd best let these boys help old Karl get all three bodies over to his cellar whilst you walk me partways up the slope. None of it's federal. So it'll be up to you and the township how you want to handle the news. Some of it's a mite delicate.''

Rothstein made no objections, and delegated some authority to one of the older townsmen in the crowd, and they went out by the back way, stepping wide of the body sprawled on the far side of the bead curtain.

Out back in the dark, Longarm paused to pee in the alley. For he was commencing to feel the way he'd been mixing his drinks on an empty stomach. Rothstein allowed he might as well piss too. As they did so together, the new constable asked where Longarm was headed once he stopped pissing.

Longarm chuckled and said, ''I told you. Up the slope.

169

I had a supper engagement with another pal that I was afraid there might not be time to keep.''

He shook the dew off the lily and added, ''Thanks to Buck Lewis I won't be as late as I feared. I reckon I owe the backshooting son of a bitch my thanks.''

Chapter 18

Constance Farnsworth answered her front door herself, her long black hair down and dressed in that same house robe as she stood in those satin mules.

As she let him into her dimly lit vestibule she gasped, "Custis! Are you all right? We heard about you shooting it out with a trio of desperados in the Hornsilver Saloon, and I naturally thought I'd seen the last of you tonight!"

Longarm took off his hat and hung it on the usual wall peg as he explained, "I never shot nobody, and as I was just now saying, it's up to the town fathers how they explain the whole affair to the *Rocky Mountain News*. So I wasn't stuck with the usual paperwork, and as you can plainly see, I didn't get shot. I'm just a mite unsteady on my feet right now because I celebrated my untimely survival with the boys on an empty stomach. I'll be all right in a minute."

She gasped, "Oh, you poor thing! Let's go right upstairs and feed you! When I thought you weren't coming I dismissed my help for the night, once I'd had a tray brought to my quarters, and as you see, planned on turning in early with a good book."

He agreed that was about what he'd have done if the shoe had been on the other foot. So she led him up her spiral staircase, and he had to fight the temptation to pinch her nice-looking bottom the way he'd seen that horny undertaker help another gal up some stairs.

Queen Victoria never would have approved, but once they got up to her bedroom suite things didn't seem all that shocking at first glance. She had this sort of sitting room between the hall door and an archway leading to what seemed a four-poster in the dim lamplight. The front chamber was more brightly lit, and a low table piled with sliced bread, cold cuts, and a tea service stood before a red leather chesterfield sofa. So he wasn't surprised that that was where they wound up as she questioned him about the gun fray she'd been able to hear clean up her way.

As she built him a hearty ham and cheese on rye sandwich he told her, "I never got to fire my own gun once. Will Posner was aiming a shotgun at me from one direction, and both Oregon John and Buck Lewis were aiming at my back from the other direction, when I ducked and the three of them shot each other."

She gasped, "Young Will Posner? Well, I never! Why on earth would that fool kid want to shoot anyone?"

Longarm sighed and said, "Because he was a fool kid. He'd somehow took it in his head that we were love rivals. We weren't. So there's no need to take another lady's name in vain."

She handed him the sandwich and began to pour them both some tea as she said, "I think I know who you mean. But I admire a man who doesn't kiss and tell."

He insisted there'd been no kissing to tell of, and bit into the sandwich. To her credit, the young widow didn't press him to talk with his mouth filled, but she seemed as antsy as Rothstein had been by the time he'd demolished another sandwich and swallowed a whole cup of tea. As she poured him another she demanded, "Tell me why that old mountain man and the foreman of the Double Seven were after you as well, Custis."

He sighed and said, "It's a long and complicated story. So I'd best start at the beginning."

He sipped some tea, leaned back, and began. "Once upon a time a silver boom bottomed out and this place called John Bull slowed down a heap as new hands were dealt, with a would-be cattle baron, a sort of grabby holding company, and a pretty lady with a railroad holding most of the face cards. I'd have never known any of this if Constable Payne hadn't wired he was holding a federal prisoner and I hadn't come up here to shake things up."

He sipped more tea and continued. "I'd have only stayed overnight and headed back to Denver with Bunny McNee if I hadn't learned just in time that he was a she."

Constance asked why he couldn't have taken along a tomboy as easily as a sissy boy.

He explained. "My boss frowns on lone deputies spending that much time alone with female suspects. You see, many a female crook has been known to charge at her trial that she was innocent, and only confessed before she'd seen a good lawyer because that mean lawman threatened to ravage her some more if she didn't let him put words in her mouth."

Constance declared, "How awful! What would you ever do if some wicked woman pulled a trick like that on you?"

To which he could only reply, "Tell my boss how sorry I was for being so dumb, I reckon. It's mortal hard to get a conviction when the defendant has compromised the arresting officer. That's what they call it when a lawman fools with a suspect. Compromising."

She set her cup aside, took his away from him, and was

suddenly in his lap with both arms around his startled shoulders as she told him in a sultry tone, "Goody! I want to compromise you!"

So he hugged her back and reeled her in so they could kiss and swab one another's tonsils with their tongues while he slid a free hand inside her house robe to discover that she wasn't wearing so much as a nightgown under it.

But as he ran his palm up the inside of a creamy thigh to where things felt warm and fuzzy, she pulled her face back just enough to giggle and say, "Not here! In my bed, the right way, you silly!"

So he swept her up in his arms and carried her the short way to one awesome amount of fun. She'd slipped out of her robe and slid a plump pillow under her voluptuous hips by the time he'd shucked his own duds fast. Then she wrapped her naked legs around his bare waist as he entered her with no shilly-shally as if they were old pals, though her innards were sweet, hot, unexplored territory to his raging erection, bless her rollicking rump.

To her credit, and unlike a lot of women, even women who'd come right out and told you they'd been married one time, Constance made no effort to explain how she'd learned to fornicate so swell. Nor did she comment on some positions *he* suggested, save to say how good they felt. But once they had to pause for their second winds long enough to share a smoke, Constance snuggled closer and said, "Now that I know you never suspected *me,* what on earth has been going on around here? Those crooks with C.C.H. had poor Gaylord murdered so he would never show us that simple trick with Wilkinson rails, right?"

Longarm placed the cheroot to her lush lips as he shook his head and said, "Forget that holding company entirely. I was just explaining to another curious kid how you start by eliminating everyone who has to be innocent. T.S. Nabors is a tight-fisted bargain hunter, but he's smart. It would have been dumb to order outsiders such as that Englishman and a federal deputy murdered when he could have had nobody but your own self disappear, at half the cost and a whole lot more discreetly. You saw yourself how easy it was to have your two-faced maid drop out of sight, and the clincher is where her body wound up.''

Constance handed the smoke back, objecting, ''Sarah was found on C.C.H. property, dear!''

He set the cheroot aside, saying, ''By C.C.H. hired help, in the hopper of a stamping mill, for Pete's sake. I saw what was left of a body run through such a process up near Deadwood a spell back. I knew who it was beforehand. It was just as well. There's no way to identify a corpse chewed to bits and sort of blended with a mess of rock dust.''

She shuddered against him—it felt swell—and said, ''Brr. I don't think I'd like to be run through a stamping mill. But you just said C.C.H. owned it, remember?''

He nodded and said, ''That's what lets 'em off. T.S. Nabors would have had to be way dumber than a mine manager ought to be if he hid a dead body in his own stamp mill and never turned on the steam engine! Think how simple it would have been for the man in charge of of the whole shebang to just reduce little Sarah to nothing anyone would ever have noticed.''

She did, but demanded, ''Then who, if not them?''

He said, ''I was able to eliminate old Jed Nolan, cheap and greedy as *he'd* be as well. He was trying to hog all the cows in this park. But he hadn't been stealing them. They were standing there in plain sight, waiting to be stolen. It's been my experience that not even a range hog steals his own cows.''

She began to toy with the hairs on his belly as she confessed he had her totally confounded.

He took her wrist to move her hand down where it might do them both more good and told her, as she took the matter in hand, to let him start from the beginning again.

She tweaked his limp member playfully and allowed she was all ears. He said he'd get her for that and continued. "Jed Nolan was planning on an even bigger herd on more open range. His foreman, Buck Lewis, was planning on stealing the herd he had and driving 'em over to another boom to sell 'em sudden at a handsome price. He'd recruited Oregon John as a guide over the mountains and that drifting badman, Quicksilver Quinn, as a badman."

"What about that mean Ginger Bancott who shot poor Gaylord?" she asked, moving her hand faster as she felt some response down yonder.

Longarm said, "Forget Ginger for now. He was just another killer on the dodge. The cow thieves never recruited him."

She started to ask who had. He warned her to hesh and went on. "Set Ginger aside for now and come with me to the Elk Rack Hotel where a wayward gal named Tess Jennings was sleeping on the sly with yet *another* drifter. We're still working on whether she'd run off from home, a husband, or a house of ill repute. She had no criminal record."

"But I *thought she was that bandit Bunny McNee!*" Constance protested.

He said, "Not so fast if you want me to get to the point in time. She wasn't Bunny McNee. The real Bunny McNee is a short soft-looking lad who may or may not be a sissy as well as a bandit. As of now, nobody on our side knows where he might really be. The so far unknown saddle tramp Tess Jennings was traveling with had her dress as a man

176

for some reason that might have made more sense to them.''

"I'll bet she was hiding out from a jealous husband!'' the young widow decided. Longarm didn't bother to say jealous idiots had been known to act scary. They'd already talked about Will Posner.

He said, ''Let's keep on eliminating. The shabby couple must've been low on money but expecting some. He might have been a gambling man, hoping his luck would change. At any rate he put her into the hotel as a single, then snuck up the service stairs after dark to steal his half of a double room. You can't hide every sin from hotel help. So they figured a young sissy boy was entertaining some brutal queer-lover, and who's going to knock on any door at a time such as that?''

She stopped beating his meat. You had to admire a gal who knew just how to get along with a man in her bed. He knew she wanted to hear the end of his story first. So he said, ''Whatever the deal, her traveling companion deserted her. He may have had to skip out on other card sharks. He might have just gotten tired of her. She wasn't all that statuesque with her shirt open. So the poor thing was stuck there, eating in her room and putting it on the hotel tab she had no way of paying. Then she finally just tried to skip. She boarded your narrow-gauge at the last moment, and might have made it if, through no fault of your own or anyone else, your combination hadn't been stopped by rocks on the tracks and backed up the grade with her, after the hotel had already spread the alarm. So Constable Payne arrested her on a charge of theft of service, and that would have cost her thirty days in the county jail if that had been the end of it.''

Constance sat up on one elbow to stare down at him with a puzzled smile as she clung to his organ-grinder, asking,

177

"But didn't you say everyone thought she was Bunny McNee?"

Longarm shook his head and said, "An eager kid deputy called Nate Rothstein thought the prisoner in the back might be the notorious Bunny McNee. The older and wiser Constable Payne knew better, whether he ever got any from her or not. But Nate Rothstein saw a resemblance to an outlaw with considerable paper hanging on him. The real Bunny McNee would be worth over a thousand dollars in various bounties, and I know for a fact that old Amos Payne was drawing less than five hundred dollars a year and had expensive habits."

She gasped. "You mean he *knew,* but hoped to collect some reward money before anyone was any the wiser? But Custis how would he get a wayward girl to go along with the charade long enough for him to collect even half that bounty money?"

Longarm dryly answered, "How else? He made a deal with her, of course. He told the desperately broke gal that he'd cut her in on the bounty money if she'd play at being Bunny McNee until he could collect it. The deal was for her to go through the whole charade, as you put it, stoutly maintaining her innocence and denying she was the real Bunny McNee whilst everyone winked, nudged, and paid off on the lying little rascal. But of course, once the bounties had been paid, and before she served any real time . . ."

"She only had to open her shirt and drop her jeans!" The naked lady in bed with him laughed.

Longarm said, "Yep. That was the plan. Then they heard Billy Vail was sending *me* instead of the original deputies assigned the chore. I don't like to brag. But I've been in the papers more than Smiley and Dutch from my home office. So Payne panicked. He figured I was chosen because I knew something. Likely something as simple as what the real Bunny McNee looked like. Payne couldn't confide in his kid deputies. None of them knew what he and the gal in the back had been planning. But he'd somehow met up with Ginger Bancott, who might have been bribing an underpaid lawman not to notice he was up this way. At any rate, he got in touch with the killer and they made yet another deal. I was saved by the simple fact that they only had a description to go by and that English civil engineer you'd hired sort of fit it.''

She gasped, "Oh, Lord, poor Gaylord! Nobody ever shot him to keep him from working for me! They shot him because they thought he was you! But wait a second, dear, didn't Constable Payne shoot Ginger Bancott for shooting you—I mean Gaylord?''

Longarm nodded curtly and said, "To silence and collect on *him*! I hope you've grasped by now that a man who'd mess with a pal's wife and put in for bounty money under false pretenses is hardly a paragon of virtue!''

She lay back down and began stroking again as she replied, "I suppose not. He sounds awfully wicked. Who was that married woman you mentioned? Was I right about Prunella Thalman?''

Longarm chuckled and said, "I don't talk about ladies who've done me no harm. The one they had locked up in that patent cell got all spooked after guns commenced to go off all around her. So she wanted out. She likely told old Amos she did before she wrote me a desperate message saying she was ready to talk.''

Constance asked, "Was that when somebody came to break out someone who they took to be Bunny McNee? Wait a moment. That won't work if her own pals knew she wasn't him, and the real Bunny McNee's pals were nowhere around here!''

Longarm hugged her closer and said, "You ought to be

their new constable. Nobody was out to bust her out. Amos Payne had to shut her up. But she was locked up for the night, guarded by a kid called Tim Keen. But Amos was his boss. So Tim naturally opened up and went back to the cell block with him when he offered some fool excuse for seeing the prisoner. Once the three of them were alone back there, Amos Payne simply drew his .45 short and shot Tess Jennings and Tim Keen in cold blood. But his twenty eight grains of powder hadn't done a tough kid all the way in yet. So as Constable Payne turned to dash out into the dark so's he could come running the other way a few moments later, the boy he'd put on the floor got his own gun out and blazed away with his .45 long. The more powerful fire blew the front door open as well. So the picture we found as the smoke was clearing fit together wrong. I might have been smarter, sooner, if those other crooks hadn't been throwing their own grit in my eyes. Nobody involved had all that much common sense. But I've noticed in the past how two dumb rascals, working at cross-purposes, can make a confounded lawman think he's up against something really slick, and speaking of slick, you're fixing to get that hand all slick and wet if you don't let me put the fool thing where it want to finish!''

So she let him, and it felt so good he decided he might as well come in her again.

Chapter 19

Sometime later down in Denver, Longarm watched and waited in Billy Vail's office as the crusty old cuss took forever to read a lot more paper than Longarm had ever handed in. Vail finally lowered it to his cluttered desk, snorted blue smoke at the younger man seated across from him in the oak-paneled back room, and declared, ''I am mad as hell and you'd better not never do it again. But fair is fair, and had Smiley and Dutch gone up yonder to transfer that fool female prisoner, we might have wound up looking awfully silly. That crooked lawman never would have ordered them killed, nobody would have felt the need to kill that runaway wife and the kid deputy, and she'd have let us put her on trial and convict her before she just laughed in our faces and bared a pair of tits the real Bunny McNee has never been accused of having!''

Longarm cocked a brow and asked, ''We know that much about the late Tess Jennings now?''

Vail nodded his bullet head. ''*You* didn't. *I* was the one who finally trailed her back to Arkansas on paper. She ran off on a hog farmer and two bitty kids with a tinhorn gambler who might or might not have been the drifter who

181

stranded her up in John Bull. Forget about her. This wicked world is as well off without the likes of her and that two-faced housemaid who almost got you killed.''

Vail blew more smoke out both nostrils and added, ''Thanks to the way some deputies from this office like to duck out on paperwork, that new young Constable Rothstein is taking the credit for solving both their murders in an election year.''

Longarm shrugged and replied, ''Hell, I'd have had to go back for the trials of them cattle thieves if I'd been any less generous with old Nate. May I *please* light my own smoke?''

Vail snapped, ''No. I told you that was an order and I meant it. That'll learn you to spill tobacco ash on my rug and grind it in with a boot heel, as if I wasn't watching!''

He glared down at the papers on his desk and said, ''Where was I? Oh, right, you say in your report to me that you're only alleging a mess of stuff instead of charging it because none of it seemed to be federal and you didn't know how the locals wanted to phrase some of it to the newspapers.''

Longarm shrugged. ''Like I said, I had no call to get myself embroiled in a stupid shouting match. All the really wicked ones had wound up dead. So justice had been served, in a sort of rough and ready fashion.''

Vail grimaced, blew more smoke, and said, ''You could have taken a tad more credit for yourself and this office without causing all that much of a fuss. The powers that be around John Bull have decided on honesty as the best policy in an election year, with justice served, the way you just said. The late Constable Payne's position ain't no political issue this coming November, and they thought they owed it to young Tim Keen's memory to record him as a hero who died at the hands of a total son of a bitch but

182

managed to take his killer with him. Nobody up that way gave a shit about a double-dealing foreman or a windy old mountain man. So they decided that cowboy, Will Posner, might as well get the credit for killing the two of them in another desperate gunfight.''

Longarm blinked, started to object, then said, ''Why not? The kid was a love-struck asshole, not a crook. Before I left I heard he had kin in the county, and he'd have been pleased as punch to see a pretty gal called Flora at his funeral in a new hat. She told us later she'd always thought him sort of dumb. But at least she was there.''

Vail grumbled, ''We'll get to all them social functions you seem to have attended up that way in a minute. Having buried them two heroic local boys with honors, and not feeling it worth their while to dig Amos Payne up and re-plant him where he belongs, in potter's field, they planted Oregon John there and sent Buck Lewis back to Texas as per request by his kin. The nicest thing about all this blood and slaughter this time is that hardly anyone is sore at you personally. Nobody but that French Sarah seemed to feel it was cruel and unusual of you to win a fair fight with Quick-silver Quinn in a reading room. Everyone else who got killed, fair or foul, got killed by somebody else. What was that about you telling them to send the bounty on Quinn to the John Bull Public School?''

Longarm shrugged and said, ''I know you frown on us federal riders putting in for bounty money, but there was a handsome reward posted on Quicksilver, dead or alive. He did die on school property, and I happen to know the school's strapped for cash. Can I go now? Or at least open the damned window, Boss?''

Vail cackled. ''You're one to talk, smoking them cheap cheroots like a Mexican! I ain't done with you yet. I'll allow that all in all things worked out better when you changed places with the deputies I had ordered up to John Bull. All's well that ends well, and we'll say no more about your report, save for the simple fact that all the events you reported transpired last week. Not *this* week. *Last* week. So how do you account for all them social gatherings and such you've been going to on our time for damn near a full week?''

Longarm said, "Damn it, Billy, if you won't let me light up in self-defense, the least you could do would be to blow that stink the other way!''

Vail took a deep drag, enveloped Longarm in a pungent cloud, and insisted, "I'm waiting!''

Longarm replied with an innocent smile, "I was stuck up in the high country waiting on a train out. Did I mention on paper how that first victim, Stanwyk, had gone up yonder to show them how to fix a mess of narrow-gauge tracks? Well, somebody else told 'em how to do it, and so the track workers had to just about take the whole railroad apart and put it back together. I *told* the owner of the line I ought to be getting on back to Denver. But I was told the trains just wouldn't be running until the owner was good and ready to start 'em up again. So there I was with no way to get home. But at least you'll see I never charged per diem to my expenses. The owner of the railroad said I could stay up there as a guest of the same, seeing it was their fault.''

Vail sat back, mollified, but muttered, "Must be fun to own your own railroad. You get to order so many folk around and . . . What's so funny, you grinning ape?''

To which Longarm could only reply, "Nothing, Boss. When you're right you're right.''

Watch for

LONGARM AND THE KANSAS KILLER

200th in the bold LONGARM series
from Jove

and

LONGARM AND THE UNWRITTEN LAW

15th in the LONGARM GIANT series

Both coming in August!

If you enjoyed this book, subscribe now and get...

TWO FREE

A $7.00 VALUE–

If you would like to read more of the very best, most exciting, adventurous, action-packed Westerns being published today, you'll want to subscribe to True Value's Western Home Subscription Service.

Each month the editors of True Value will select the 6 very best Westerns from America's leading publishers for special readers like you. You'll be able to preview these new titles as soon as they are published, *FREE* for ten days with no obligation!

TWO FREE BOOKS

When you subscribe, we'll send you your first month's shipment of the newest and best 6 Westerns for you to preview. With your first shipment, two of these books will be yours as our introductory gift to you absolutely *FREE* (a $7.00 value), regardless of what you decide to do. If

you like them, as much as we think you will, keep all six books but pay for just 4 at the low subscriber rate of just $2.75 each. If you decide to return them, keep 2 of the titles as our gift. No obligation.

Special Subscriber Savings

When you become a True Value subscriber you'll save money several ways. First, all regular monthly selections will be billed at the low subscriber price of just $2.75 each. That's at least a savings of $4.50 each month below the publishers price. Second, there is never any shipping, handling or other hidden charges—*Free home delivery*. What's more there is no minimum number of books you must buy, you may return any selection for full credit and you can cancel your subscription at any time. A TRUE VALUE!

WESTERNS!

NO OBLIGATION

Mail the coupon below

To start your subscription and receive 2 FREE WESTERNS, fill out the coupon below and mail it today. We'll send your first shipment which includes 2 FREE BOOKS as soon as we receive it.

Mail To: **True Value Home Subscription Services, Inc. P.O. Box 5235**
120 Brighton Road, Clifton, New Jersey 07015-5235

YES! I want to start reviewing the very best Westerns being published today. Send me my first shipment of 6 Westerns for me to preview FREE for 10 days. If I decide to keep them, I'll pay for just 4 of the books at the low subscriber price of $2.75 each; a total $11.00 (a $21.00 value). Then each month I'll receive the 6 newest and best Westerns to preview Free for 10 days. If I'm not satisfied I may return them within 10 days and owe nothing. Otherwise I'll be billed at the special low subscriber rate of $2.75 each; a total of $16.50 (at least a $21.00 value) and save $4.50 off the publishers price. There are never any shipping, handling or other hidden charges. I understand I am under no obligation to purchase any number of books and I can cancel my subscription at any time, no questions asked. In any case the 2 FREE books are mine to keep.

Name

Street Address   Apt. No.

City   State   Zip Code

Telephone

Signature
(if under 18 parent or guardian must sign)

Terms and prices subject to change. Orders subject
to acceptance by True Value Home Subscription
Services, Inc.

11655-6